THE CHINA DOLL CONSPIRACY

Little Miss Dangerous

ALAN PETERS

First Edition

NEWMAN SPRINGS PUBLISHING
320 Broad Street
Red Bank, NJ 07701

First originally published by Newman Springs Publishing 2022

Although some of the characters in this novel may resemble actual living people, they are strictly fictitious, modified in name and character to any actual living people.

ISBN 978-1-68498-711-5 (Paperback)
ISBN 978-1-68498-712-2 (Digital)

Printed in the United States of America

To my parents who taught me right from wrong and to my brother who pushed the envelope right toward wrong.

To my wife, an American citizen immigrant from the Philippines, who showed me what hard work is and is an award-winning nurse in ICU which she very humbly accepted.

Man
Woman

THE CHINA DOLL CONSPIRACY: THE MAIN CHARACTERS

Thomas—sixth, later eighth degree black belt sensei who has trained many of the team to different levels of black belt

Greater—second degree (nidan) black belt and an active cop in a small New Jersey town

Alex—second degree (nidan) black belt, chemist, and criminalistics professor pursuing Chinese ladies for a wife

Dennis—second degree (nidan) black belt operating two dojos in New Jersey; also uses middle name Ed

Doc—first degree (shodan) black belt orthodontist trained by Thomas

Ho—a renegade kung fu Shaolin priest of high rank; skilled in Mandarin, Tagalog, and English

Van deGraff brothers—two black belt assistants to Lenten

Lenten—an eighth degree black belt who is the coordinator of all operations stationed in Taipei, Taiwan

Ping—the CCP chairman and PRC head of state and creator of the China doll conspiracy

Susan—China doll #1 in Nutley, NJ

Ling—China doll #2 in Staten Island, NY

Qing—China doll #3 in Brooklyn, NY

INTRODUCTION

The honey trap has been in use since Adam and Eve. Eve established the precedent when she asked Adam to take a bite of an apple from the tree of good and evil, the God-forbidden tree of knowledge. Adam, seduced by Eve, thus started the downfall of mankind. Evicted from the perfect life of supply and leisure from the garden of Eden, descendants of Adam and Eve were doomed to a life of hard work to obtain the necessities of life. Even the snake was sentenced to a life of crawling on his belly for his tempting of Eve.

Life is hard all but for that one bite of the forbidden apple. Women must bear great pain to birth a child. Man must work his fingers to the bone to support his family, and sometimes Eve too needed to take up the cross of hard work to assist in providing for the family.

The honey trap has been used time and time again by governments, organizations, and individuals to redirect the path of men (and women) toward illicit goods or decisions that were of outright or questionable illegality to placate the spouse. Men, more often than women, fell into the honey trap.

A few examples might be a Chinese woman starting an affair with a congressman to obtain military or government classified information. Relaxing after sex, the man may divulge most anything having been pleasured by the China doll. He may even come to confide in her after a while. Another China doll could "work" her way to a key position on Wall Street "earning" a millionaire lifestyle using her mind but mostly her body. However, the more sinister dolls may report their newly gleaned knowledge to the Chinese government (CCP of the PRC). This would give China a distinct advantage in economic and military areas and be very detrimental to the United

States. The dolls were part of the plan to replace the United States as the leader of the world.

This story runs along similar lines of deceit and subterfuge. The goal here is to use the honey trap to terminate important, powerful, or brilliant Americans. One fictitious American named Alexander Supenski finds himself lured by more than one honey trap, Chinese dolls programmed to destroy him through sex and intimacy. Once made complacent and relaxed in the apparent LTR or NSA situation, a terminating agent takes over. Ultimately, the Chinese government who trained the dolls will take over the beautiful United States without a full-armed conflict. Long-term planning is their goal, and failure is not an option. The dolls used were trained by the government which holds the doll's family hostage as insurance against breakaways or noncompliance to their plan.

All names and characters are fictitious even if some may appear quite familiar to the readers. No attempt is being made to dishonor an entire race of people. Like all nations including the USA, there are some very bad people lacking conscience, ethics, or morality that are unrestrained in their behavior toward others. In the end, as in this story, the antagonist will lose, and many victims will survive wiser for the attempted personal coup.

1

SETTING THE STAGE

DF: oriental, 5'4", 120 #, pretty, educated
ISO SWPM, well educated
6'+, handsome for LTR

Is there anything more beautiful than a Chinese girl with perfect oriental features? Alex mused to himself. Alex Supenski, PhD physical chemist, accomplished both academically and industrially with journal articles, presentations, and patents, just couldn't seem to accomplish finding the right woman. His former girlfriend, also a chemist, was a New Yorka who he had been engaged to for almost three years. She continued to irritate him with her lack of cultcha and class inherited from her two very much-hedonistic parents. *Why did I continue to drive over one hundred miles across twenty dollars' worth of toll bridges to be with a woman whom I stopped loving years ago?* he thought. *For a smart guy, that sounds pretty stewpit, I mean stupid. Long Islandese was destroying my vocabulary too.* Why is it that when you associate with people who are self-centered, lazy, sloppy, careless, and genuinely obnoxious, sometimes you tend to acquire the same demeanor? It's got to be entropy; there's no other excuse for it. It is the natural order of things to be disordered. *That really sounds crazy. I hope I'm not losing it...again.* Nah. All PhD chemists start off in life a little crazier than normal people; otherwise they wouldn't spend all those hours alone studying their asses off to get their degrees to make chicken feed after graduation.

Remember the good old days when you got to talk, that is, communicate—no, it was more like yelling and screaming at each other than seeing who could slam dunk the telephone receiver first on the "opponent." What a wonderful relationship that was. Actually, at the beginning it was pretty good with just going out and having some fun than continuing the fun at night in the sexual arena. That part I really couldn't complain about. The girl may have been an idiot, but sexually, she was better than okay.

Back in '92 she really went off the deep end with her idiotic behavior in Lake Tahoe. While trying to locate his niece, the ever-smiling and happy daughter he never had, who he was there to give away as a flower child kind of bride, Ms. New Yorka, Becky, his fiancée, decides that she wants to play the slots on the Nevada side of Tahoe. After threatening to leave her there to walk back to the motel, she finally relents and tags along. That was the last straw in a seemingly endless chain of aggravating events that led to the final and permanent breakup. *There will be no marriage to this woman because in less than two months of her day-to-day shit, I would have to kill her* (figuratively speaking).

Thus began the search for the right girl that led to a complicated web of investigative work which uncovered the China doll conspiracy launched by Beijing by those who both admired and envied the USA and sought ways to destroy its super power status and replace it with itself. Chairman Ping coveted all those materials assets and pictured himself in a multimillion dollar home in the Hamptons with a dozen concubines, a stretch limo in the summer, and a stretch Navigator in the winter. All the amenities of the rich and famous including some big-busted American women to play with. Why is it that many Chinese women have such small breasts? Is it genetics or environment and diet—enough to suck on but a molehill with a tiny nipple on it when compared to the typical abudanza American woman?

So Alex begins looking for the right woman in the personal ads. Why not? His philosophy concerning breasts is that any more than a hand or mouthful is excess mass just hanging out with nothing to do but envy the part in the mouth or hand. After fifteen years of karate training and graduate school with fellow students being mostly oriental or Indian, he surmised that Eastern women usually make better wives than Western women, and many tolerate virtually anything to keep family together, especially Chinese women. Could it have anything to do with the fact that they have been treated like shit by Chinese men for the last two thousand years or so? They are certainly eager to meet Western men. Just check the internet and you'll find thousands of women looking for Western husbands. *Sounds good to me. I'll skip over all the ads with the letter* W_*in them for "white," as in SWPW, i.e., single white professional woman—like my ex-girlfriend. Thanks, but no thanks* (as the song says, "American Woman, stay away from mehee"). The Asian and oriental ads will be perused since these girls have a reputation for being more cooperative, aka subservient, and letting their husband make most of the important decisions. *That sure wasn't Becky's way. She even argued with me about the color of a carpet once that I wanted to buy for my house (which never became our house). I told her that white carpets get dirty too fast and need to be cleaned a lot.* To a normal woman, this would fall into the category of common sense, but not to Becky. And guess who would be cleaning the carpet, certainly not Miss Lazy-ass. *I couldn't take her bickering and gave in, regretting the purchase of that carpet ever since.* Definitely skip the SWF ads.

Alex peruses the ads and stumbles upon the following: DF, oriental, 5'4", 120#, pretty, educated ISO SWPM, well educated, 6'+, handsome for LTR. Translation: Divorced oriental Female In Search Of Single White Professional Male for Long Term Relationship. *This girl is looking for me, Alex Supenski.* So at $1.99 per minute, he listens to her voice greeting. She has a petite, sweet voice like a little girl and speaks of complete commitment to serving her man in every way emphasizing loyalty and love and family and apple pie and all that other BS, but somehow her sweet voice sounds 100 percent sincere and truthful (BIG mistake). *How could this little gal possibly hurt anyone? She sounds so sweet that I may have to wait until I marry her before she'll have sex with me. She's looking for me, and she has just got to be a gorgeous little China doll!*

Convinced that this girl would really love her one and only man, respect him, maybe even worship him, he decides to leave a message with his description and telephone number again at $1.99 a minute. However, this is his first experience with the voice mailbox system, so naturally the message is fubar because he is super-nervous. Round two: he leaves a second version of the message which sounds roughly like he is at least a little less hyper. "Hi, Susan! My name is Alex. I am a PhD chemist, 6'3" tall, 220 lbs. (a white lie by 15 lbs.). Your ad and voice message sounded very much like the girl I am looking for to marry. My phone number is xxx-yyy-zzzz, and I would love to talk with you, and I look forward to meeting you. Hope to hear from you soon. Bye."

Now that he left a message, he ruminates about what he said and should have said. *How will I sound to her? She probably won't even call, so don't sweat it.* Then his conscience kicks in. *Hey, Alex, hello!* D *means divorced, and you are more or less a strict Catholic. What the hell are you doing? You can't marry her, and you can't just go out with her for sex because that would be fornication for you and adultery for her, and you know what the Man said about adulterers and fornicators.* Then logic kicks in. *Back off, Jack. Take it easy, Mon. I'm not marrying her yet, just meeting her if I'm lucky enough to have her call me, which she probably won't. Besides, only in my mind have I gotten any poontang yet, so, so far, only venial sins. How can you visualize sex with someone you've never seen? I can do it, a consequence of my overactive imagination as a scientist. Like I said, she probably won't even call, so slow down your panic disordered brain.*

Although a PhD physical chemist conjures up the epitome of a nerd, Alex certainly strays radically from that picture. He bought a candy apple red 1977 Kawasaki KZ-650-4 new for $1815 and used to ride it eighty miles a day on the GSP to work every day. Occasionally he would crank it out and dust somebody who thought his or her new Corvette was untouchable. He even dusted a few forty-thousand-dollar Porsches with his Japanese crotch rocket, which cost less than 5 percent of the Porsche. When the weather really turned to crap, he would drive his '84 dark blue 4WD Nissan long-bed truck with matching deep blue cap. Blue was the key word; everything he bought that cost some real bucks was blue. Even his old college alma mater colors were blue and white, midnight blue metal flake sky blue. Blue oxford shirts, faded blue denims, blue toothpaste, a diamond mist metallic blue Mazda Miata—there is no end to the blue things this guy had. The one major item recently purchased costing almost ten grand that wasn't blue was his '96 Honda VT1100 Shadow, a Harley wannabe; it was purple and white because they didn't make a blue one. Harley wannabe or not, it still dusted a few Harleys, but not by the distance that the KZ did with one-half the engine size of the Hog. Alex would have bought a Hog, but he felt that he would rather be riding the bike than fixing it, and the rice burners had a reputation for running forever on a diet of regular gas and an occasional oil change. The VT1100 sounded a little like a Harley, but the KZ sounded more like an old Singer sewing machine until you got it above 6000 rpm. Then it didn't have any audible sound at all to anyone sitting in the riding position. An engine speed of 6000 rpm on the Kaw was only 70 mph and would be red line on an HD at maybe 120 mph. High revs and maximum compression ratio requires a lot of precise machine work taking the patience of an oriental culture thousands of years old. Americans want it now or, better yet, ten minutes ago. Of course, if you wanted to tow a trailer, get the torque Hog. But if you want to travel fast and light near the speed of light (sound, maybe not even), use the KZ.

Right out of the crate, Alex took it out onto the Palisades Interstate Parkway heading downstate toward the GWB and NYC. With no one around in the early hours of a glittering, twenty-four-karat golden sunrise, he pushed it up to ninety-five, and all he could hear was a fading high-frequency engine pitch that disappeared into silence at about eighty. There was still plenty of throttle left too! That's what one thousand eight hundred bucks bought in June of 1976.

Professor Supenski (his students called him Dr. S) also studied four forms of Okinawan karate lumped together into a system called Goshen-Do Karate-Do Kyokai (then later to Shito-Ryu) for fifteen years achieving the rank of nidan or second degree black belt. So at forty-seven years old, 6'3" and 190 lbs. (ahem) at the time, he was a formidable sparring partner, to say the least. Of course there were always the more senior students and the *dai sempai*, a 5'6" cop from the local town of Fair Lawn, New Jersey, who could kick his big ass in short order with his speed and focused punch kick combinations. Then there were the Van deGraff brothers, sons of a Hawthorne police chief, who could first kill you then bury you since one was a state cop and the other was an undertaker. Also training in Supenski's home dojo was "Doc," a dentist black belt capable of removing your teeth in one way and replacing them in another.

In any event, he prided himself in being in great condition and never even took so much as an aspirin into the sanctuary of his body until after he acquired panic disorder (now under control) that virtually exiled him to his living quarters for nearly ten years. After being released from PD with medication, his outlook softened toward different people. One example was tattoos. He viewed them as an unnatural decoration of a perfect body loaned to him by his Maker for his journey through life but respected the rights of others who liked tattoos. Alex didn't want to look tough on the exterior; he wanted to be humble, tough inside but friendly and soft-spoken on the outside so as not to alienate people. Now all that he was and was not waited nervously but confidently from one day to the next for that important phone call from a sweet, demure petite Chinese girl. When it came to most aspects of life, Alex was realistic; when it came to women, he was ludicrously naïve and trusting. This first escapade into the world of the communist Chinese women was about to open his eyes wider than a gymnast could spread her legs, and spreading legs was also what he had somewhat in mind.

2

THE PHONE CALL: PRELUDE TO THE FIRST MEETING

Two days after Alex left his jittery message, a gal with a petite and sweet voice calls. Her name is Sue. He found out later that Sue was an Americanization of Shui, the girl's real Chinese name. They talked for about forty-five minutes as she kind of interviews him, who is now convinced more than ever that this China doll is the one for him. Then after that first phone conversation, she calls him <u>every</u> night. This seems quite out of the ordinary to him, but he writes it off as a cultural difference that he is not familiar with rather than using it as an insight into the type of woman he is dealing with. Big mistake number one, and it was going to cost him dearly in the very near future too. But it was going to cost many other men even more dearly to an extent that was unimaginable upon first impressions of this demure, sweet Chinese gal.

At the end of the Friday night phone conversation of the same week, Alex arranges to meet her at a shopping center in Nutley, about a fifty-mile trek for him but apparently not far from where Sue is living. Time: noon tomorrow, Saturday, high noon with the same flavor of the notorious gun battle that took place in Tombstone, Arizona. With a pedestal level of hope and an angelic image of a beautiful oriental matching her voice, Saturday finds him going to the Nutley shopping center. He parks his blue Nissan long-bed truck near the marquee about one hundred feet to the shopping center's main entrance. As usual, he is early and starts to walk toward the entrance dressed in a dark blue overcoat with a gray fur collar holding a small box of chocolates in his hand with a shimmering red rose carefully secured to his lapel. This is the sign of recognition that they had agreed upon the previous night. Scanning the parking lot and entrance, Alex starts the search for his exotic beauty. *I wonder which one of these Asian girls she is and how she looks compared to what I think she looks like*, he thinks to himself. However, after she fails to show by twelve forty-five, his hopes begin to fade like the intermittent sunlight when the sun dips below the horizon. He can't believe he is being stood up by such a trustworthy, sweet girl. Retrieving her phone number from his well-aged tan wallet, he calls her from an open-air blue phone booth outside the shopping center. After several busy signals, he finally gets through. He hears "Hello," but it is a weak hello wrought with tears and upset. "Hello? Susan?" He exhales.

"Yes," she strains to say through a valley of tears.

"This is Alex, the guy on the phone last night. Are you coming to meet me?" he asks her. She tells him that she just had a fight with her ex-husband (living nearby whom Alex will ultimately realize that he is more than just her ex-husband). Alex replies, "I am sorry to hear that. Are you okay?"

Sue answers, "I'll be all right."

Then he sheepishly suggests, "Would you rather not meet today and arrange for another time?"

Susan quickly responds, "No, no. I'm sorry. Give me ten minutes to get dressed and I'll be there. How to recognize you?"

Alex describes himself. "I'm a big guy wearing a blue overcoat with a gray collar with the red rose in the lapel. I'll be waiting at the Acme."

"Okay, see you then," she says and he hears the distinctive click of the replaced receiver.

Alex's ruminating begins: *Oh boy, a fine day I picked to meet this girl. And what's this ex-husband shit, anyway? Whatever happened to the famous Alex creed, "I won't go out with anyone whom I work with, am related to, or is married"? But she's not married any longer. Any longer? What about the local ex-husband? I can read the headlines now: "Caucasian college professor tortured and murdered by deranged ex-husband of Chinese woman." A love triangle where I lose to a Chinese kung fu expert in a fight to the death. Wait a minute, son, this isn't the sixteenth century, and more than likely this ex whatever is probably not a Shaolin priest but some scrawny 90 lb. weakling. Yeah... that's the spirit, stay positive. Besides, you already violated two parts of the Alex creed by dating a third and fifth female cousin and going out with that Iranian graduate student that worked with you in the same research group at the State University. You're just looking for a reason to split because you're scared. A nidan scared? What would sensei think of you splitting and not facing your fears? Probably throw you out of the dojo. I'm staying here, and I will meet her. Period.*

About ten minutes seem to go by (it was really more like thirty minutes; you know women), and a petite oriental drives up in a light gray Nissan Sentra. Alex walks up to the car and says, "Susan?"

She says, "Are you Alex?"

"Yep, that's me. Why don't you park your car in my space and we'll go in my truck and have lunch."

Susan agrees and follows him back to his parking space with her Sentra. Alex jumps into his truck, cranks the starter bringing the four cylinders to life. She drives her car to where he pulls his truck out and pulls in. While getting into the truck, Alex sneaks a look at her from a distance of about two feet. She truly is a doll—medium-short black silky hair, a medium complexion with beautiful smooth skin, and gorgeous almond eyes, brown or nearly black. She is trim and neatly proportional in her features and is wearing a white embroidered blouse buttoned to the top (very proper, he thinks) and a dark green suede miniskirt. Her legs sport black fishnet nylons, and she at once looks demure yet sleazy. Her exposed legs are very sexy, and Alex finds it difficult to keep his eyes from focusing too long on them. She has a very pretty face with nice white teeth but with a space between the two top front-most teeth that lends a little of a childlike appearance to her. What a beautiful Chinese doll; her radically slanted dark eyes are exquisitely exotic and sexy yet extreme in some unspeakable way. Her overall appearance is quite pleasing, yet he hears a voice inside himself asking, *What is wrong with this picture?*

Handing the small box of chocolates and a single long-stem red rose to her, Alex says, "These are for you."

"Thank you," the demure little Susan squeaks out.

Then Alex asks her, "Do you like Italian food? There's a restaurant near here called Rosa Linda's where we can have lunch."

"Yes, that would be good," she answers.

So Alex and his doll from the PRC chat lightly, both a little nervous while he navigates the back roads of Clifton to Linda's. Much of the "all about me, all about you" conversation has already taken place on the phone over the last several evenings. However, to avoid those dangerous nerve-racking lulls in the conversation, Alex starts in on the nickel tour of the neighborhood about streets that are zipping by the windows of the truck. "I was born not too far from here in Passaic, and I used to work for a small printing company here in Clifton during summer break when I was a junior in college." Alex delivered packages of printed goods to many locations in the Clifton area, so he knew the territory well even twenty-seven years later. It seems that a delivery person learns virtually every nook and cranny of all the towns he travels through while making his assigned stops. This includes finding out where the best hangouts and good restaurants are. About two dozen years back, he delivered beer and learned every watering hole in Port Jervis, NY, like he had been born there and not in St. Mary's hospital in Passaic.

In those days on the screaming yellow Rheingold trucks was painted, "The beer with the ten-minute head," a source of countless profane jokes. Port Jervis is an extremely old town on a three-state line (NY, NJ, and PA), and the beer always was delivered and stored down in the cellars. Those cellar floors took to the wheels of a beer-loaded handcart like a fly to fly paper being essentially dirt well-limed to keep the rat population at bay. The entrance to the cellars looked like they had been created by dynamite with the stone stairs being built from the concrete pieces of the blasted-out walls. Here, Alex encountered the two deliveryman nightmares: uneven rise of each step and a low, less than six-foot ceiling. Frequently the cases or barrels of beer ended up on the dirt floor scattered widely. At least it scared the rats away.

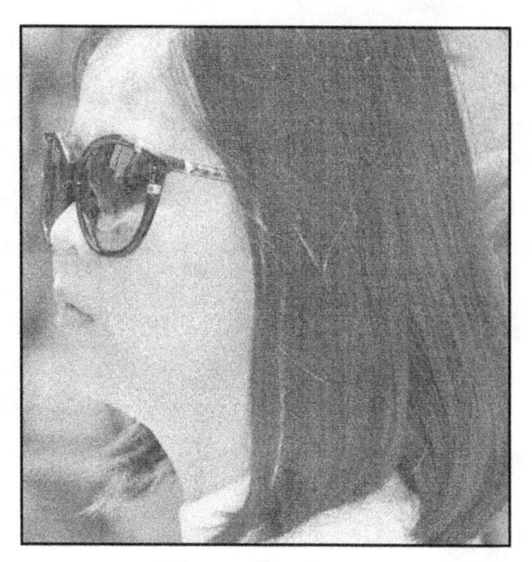

Zhong Shui Long

The couple finally reaches Linda's Ristorante, and it looks as empty as the evacuated main street of the urban renewal project in Newburgh. Alex parks in the designated lot and switches off the four cylinders. He walks over to the passenger side of his truck carefully avoiding some residual snow and ice characteristic of this time of year in NJ. Trying to be a perfect gentleman, he opens Susan's door, and his hand is met by her hand as he navigates her past the dangerous ice capable of taking out a person as quickly as it sunk the *Titanic*. A chill runs up his spine, and a nerve in his left leg close to his groin pulsates coincident with her very touch. She is very pretty and exotic looking but dressed quite Western; there's some inconsistency here. Her demure face, sweet, soft, childlike voice and personality are in conflict with her sexy skirt, black patterned nylons, and somewhat sleazy but neat appearance. His banal coarse nature tells him that he is with a petite nice piece of ass and is stimulated by these thoughts and those nylons. He begins to think that maybe he could "get some" before he marries her after all. That's a silly thought; she has already been married, so she must know what sex is. It's not like she is a virgin with zero experience, especially since there's nearly two billion people in China. Seems like all they do over there is screw and have babies.

They approach the side entrance of Linda's hoping that the *ristorante* is open for business. To him, *ristorante* seems to be just a word that allows the Italian restaurants to raise the price of a bowl of spaghetti ($0.50/lb. at ShopRite) to twelve bucks. As the door swings open widely with a firm push, Susan enters and heads pop up as the handful of people therein are attuned to her beauty, exoticness, and sleaze all at once. The couple chooses a booth near the entrance, and they scrutinize each other thoroughly while attempting not to stare. Alex thinks, *I can't believe my eyes that this girl is so attractive yet petite and well mannered—so apparently sweet and shy with the face of a little girl and the body of a woman (aka little miss dangerous). Uh-oh! Get the pedestal.*"

Susan suggests to Alex that he order for her, so he orders two chicken Parmesan dinners just loving how she let him make this little decision. *A little submissive to me already.* That was the main problem with Ms. New Yorka—she had to have her say in everything, even little bullshit things like the color of a rug, a rug that she would never get to walk on in a house that she would never get to live in. He never liked that about her because it reminded him of her mother who was a Jewish princess (even though she wasn't Jewish), always being catered to by her truly Jewish father, a sweet, nice guy who never learned to say no.

"What part of China are you from?" he asks.

"I am from a city called Tianjin near Beijing," answers little Miss Dangerous.

"Would you write your full Chinese name for me using kanji characters?" he requests.

Susan tears a piece of the paper from the place mat and scribbles the three pictorial characters which she loosely translates as Jong Shoe Lou in pinyin pronunciation but written as Zhong Shui Long. Her name *Shui* she has Americanized to *Sue*, so she's Sue Long.

Lunch arrives, and Alex clears his plate like a hurdler over the high fences, but his petite, little doll only bird-consumes her lunch. Coffee arrives, and she adds five bags of sugar. He thinks, *That's highly unusual, five sugars? I use five sugars, but I'm easily twice her size, both sideways and volume-wise. We are both heavy sugar users—something in common! Eureka!* Susan is also a college graduate, and her father is a retired chemistry professor in Tianjin (so she says)—no wonder she agreed to meet me. As a couple, they are pulling down some strange looks from the other Americans; they look at him then at her then at him again but say nothing. He thinks out loud, "*Hey. Be careful what you say to me! I may be a psychotic serial killer. Screw'em, I couldn't care less what they think. I really like this sexy little gal.*"

The check comes, and Sue offers to pay half, but Alex refuses and insists it's the man's obligation in this country. Then he excuses himself to make a pit stop at the john. He set himself up at the urinal and quips to his Johnson down below, "You may get to see some action a lot sooner than you think, Johnson." Unbeknownst to Alex as he relieves himself at this time is the depth of understatement this will turn out to be very soon, developing with the second date and nearly exploding on the third date. He finishes taking care of business and leaves the men's room meeting Sue at the exit. They walk back to the truck and get in then proceed back to the starting point, Acme. Alex parks the truck and walks Sue to her gray Nissan and asks her, "May I kiss you goodbye?" while pointing to his cheek.

Sue smiles, indicative of a yes, and after the one millisecond kiss, he then asks her if he can call her again. She is quite amenable to the idea of more dates and nods yes. He follows her out of the parking lot and for a few blocks until she turns right. She waves to him as she turns, and he and Johnson are in seventh heaven. But now his super-religious conscience kicks in, and a moral dilemma is about to ensue.

3

TRAINING—ONE YEAR EARLIER, HUNAN PROVINCE, PRC

Susan is sitting quietly, dressed in baggy khaki undergarments amidst forty-nine other "China dolls" in a small, damp, and cold room two stories underground. It had a cement floor like a prison ward, and its walls are adorned with brainwashing posters proclaiming the ultimate Chinese takeover of the United States of America, to be accomplished without a single shot being fired if possible.

A military colonel, Yang, herself dressed in a faded green uniform reminiscent of what you might find in an army-navy store in NYC, leads the chorus in Mandarin.

"We are the future of America. We will accelerate its rotting from within using our minds and our bodies. The ultimate victory of the People's Republic is worth dying for. Long live Chairman Ping!" On and on goes the sickening cadence, as it gets progressively louder.

Many of the girls were teenagers as young as thirteen. They were selected for their nice bodies and cute childlike faces and their appeal tested on Western men held captive in the country-wide dungeons. The girls are shivering since they are only wearing underwear as a means to burn into their consciousness that their bodies are their tools, their vehicles of destruction to help a country on the brink of total immorality go over the edge and proceed to enslavement.

To ensure that none of the girls become renegades once in America, Ping has ordered the arrest and determent of a close relative chosen for their particular attachment to each of the young women. Susan has a nine-year-old son, Tao, who is being kept at a secret "school" in the Himalayas in Chinese-occupied Tibet. If Susan does not achieve her quota of men, her parents will also be locked away in some shithole buried deep in northern China. To ensure success, one of Ping's Secret Police Monitors (SPMs) will pose as the estranged (ex) husband who will finish the projects started by each girl if the girl screws up and who will report her weekly progress directly to Ping through a secure integrated internet connection to his office. These are tied in to the various underground rooms in Chinatowns throughout the USA where the SPMs check in weekly.

Yang, looking more like a small ugly man than a woman, orders the girls to stand up and raise their T-shirts. It looks like a small boob competition, with the spherical symmetry of boobs so perfect that you could swear that the maker constructed them with a compass. As she passes each girl, she is handed a spring-loaded retainer by her assistant that she clips on each nipple to demonstrate a fraction of the pain that each girl will receive if she fails. If the girl removes either or both retainers, she is immediately taken out by the male sentries and caned like a common criminal (whipping leaves marks). No one is allowed to make a sound, although the pain has occasionally caused some frail girls to pass out. They are left there to revive themselves, retainers being removed, and face additional punishment if they are late for their next "class," usually language class. (This consists of the present-day colloquial and slang words and proper pronunciation of English in America.) Torturing and subjugating these women is natural for the Chinese. China never did have much respect for its women, and their men have always used them without regard for their health or condition. This program merely carries on this sadistic Chinese tradition of treating their women like shit. Chinese women in their late thirties and early forties are mostly divorced. Their ex-husbands trade them in for a fresh twenty-something pieces of poontang with much more juicy and tasty flowers than the old ladies whom they dumped.

This group of fifty China dolls was being prepared for implantation in the northeast United States. Many Chinese already resided in the area near Rutgers, the state University of New Jersey, since it was a very popular and well-known school in China. Most Americans wouldn't notice the slight increase in their number caused by these walking time bombs, aka honey traps, ready to snap and seize hold of any man who fancied a taste of their exotic beauty.

One of the other girls was a tall, slender model in Shanghai before Ping "recruited" her for his devious conspiracy. This girl, Qing, was not purely Chinese by virtue of a Russian grandmother. Standing 5'7" but weighing only 90 lbs., she towered over the other 5'2" to 5'4" ladies. Unlike Susan who was cute pretty, she was a beautiful, mature woman. Her workouts at the gym and swimming pool gave her body a nice tone and balance. Alex would ultimately get to meet her too. Qing's mother was being held in Tibet, caged like a common wild beast as insurance that Qing would cooperate with demon Ping's program. She had the quintessential Chinese woman's nearly flat chest with large milkless nipples. Qing had to throw out her chest to even look like a 32A. Her allurement would be her long silky, smooth legs and flexibility usually only attained by an Olympic gymnast. She could straddle a man in virtually any position to tempt him to destroy himself by entering her. And who wouldn't want to, with her beauty and "desire to have a baby" with no strings attached to the man took her baited gang hook? She would be based in Brooklyn, NYC.

Ling, another girl assigned to the east coast, was very cute, pretty, and younger than Qing and Shui. Extremely flat-chested, her magnetism consisted of being a very intelligent PhD who immediately expressed a desire to have lots of sex in order to inject her deadly venom. This irresistible combination of brains and great sexual appetite was designed for the well-educated American males (typically professors) who would find it hard to resist her preppy appearance looking like the sweet girl next door, only with silky black hair and pretty almond eyes. She had a seven-year-old daughter, Nanchi, from whom she could receive censored letters during her training at the dingy underground facility. Nanchi was attending the same school in Tibet as Tao, Susan's nine-year-old son. Ling was going to Staten Island where she was employed as a librarian in a small college where many American professors congregated.

Each girl would be set up with a counterfeit permanent green card, history, and identity once she reached America. Certain high officials in the INS (immigration) became very cooperative with Ping's agents once they were informed that they would be shark meat in the Atlantic Ocean should they decide to be a whistleblower. The ten-thousand-dollar "speaking fee" also made these deals a no-brainer.

There were fifty girls for each state for a total of two thousand five hundred "trainees." Each girl had a very aggressive quota of contaminating twenty-five persons per year, roughly one every two weeks. Although bisexuality was frowned upon, all the girls knew that if it helped them meet their quota or exceed the expectations of the chairman, it was condoned. Other than being pretty Chinese ladies, the girls differed in many ways: age, height, weight, etc. with somewhat chubby girls a welcome part of the conspiracy since Ping himself liked a tight fit as did most Chinese men. American men are drawn to big breasts, beauty, and nice asses in a woman, but Chinese men seek out convenience and pleasure, and fat definitely adds to the pleasure part. Ping would frequently say, "Perfect woman is tight fit and soft like pillow," when he spoke of chubby ladies.

Different as they were, the ladies all had one dangerous thing in common, one implanted attribute that made them as lethal as a scorpion rearing up its back to sting. Each doll was absolutely positive in the modified western blot test. Each and every girl carried a lab-developed lethal form of syphilis and was a carrier time bomb. Carefully crafted, this form of syphilis affected Caucasians only being benign to the dolls. Ping's army of a mere two thousand five hundred could soon do what no nation on earth was ever able to do with all the firepower in the world. It could defeat the last greatest power on earth, America, by rotting and destroying it from the inside. All that was needed was the condom-less cooperation of the already promiscuous American male. To Ping, it was a done deal. China was good to go.

4

SOMEWHERE IN TIBET ON THE NEPALESE BORDER

Tibet had been occupied and controlled by Chinese forces since shortly after WW II. A beautiful country with somewhat primitive people, it borders southern China, Bhopal, and Nepal. Many draft-dodger turned hippies came here looking for the truth and the essence of life during the Vietnam War. They refused to fight because it was illegal for the US to be there, and it was a civil war between North and South Vietnam like the American Civil War in many respects. When the very unselective Selective Service System called these men to be indentured slaves of the US government, many split to Canada, Europe, and this part of Asia. Nepal and Tibet were favorite destinations since many believed that Buddhism was their answer in their search for truth. It was the home of the enlightened one, the Dalai Lama (now exiled in India). He was the austere centerpiece of Buddhism advocating an existence of meditation and peace, complete nonviolence in answer to conflict, hence the reluctance of the Tibetans to use force to expel the Chinese. The Chinese are predominantly religionless with 8 percent Buddhist but with most adherents to the peaceful principles of Confucius and Lao Tzu. However, they see no contradiction in using violence, destruction, and death to get what they want, like Tibet for instance. This is mirrored in the West by Christians who will step over a homeless man in order to get into their limos.

In Ping's world, Buddhism was merely another tool to be used to accomplish his conspiracies around the world. If it conflicted with his desires in any way, he would just ignore those precepts.

Here in Tibet was the school where Susan's son, Tao, and Ling's seven-year-old daughter, Nanchi, were being educated into the Karl Marx version of Buddhism and loyalty to China. Temples adorned with brilliant colors, layers of gold, red, and green having roofs of cascading shingles were being desecrated by the Chinese who used them for everything from schools to brothels. After all, religion never worked for Ping's interests, so he took what he could use for his devious purposes. Some of the temples were built on high overhanging cliffs in the Himalayas. These were used for the troublesome students who could be tossed down twelve thousand feet if they showed any dissatisfaction with their educational program. The inaccessible valley below became a graveyard and grim reminder of what independent thought could earn you here.

Susan's son had been moved here after her six weeks without a "kill" in America, so they told her. This non-kill was Alex, that determined and well-prepared to survive American professor she was falling in love with but would shortly defer to her ex (SPM) for termination since she was unsuccessful.

Tao inherited his mother's resilience and passion. He didn't help his own destiny by referring to Ping as the pile of rotting yak dung. Tao heard this description of Ping from some American hostages held in Tibet along with his grandparents, Susan's mother and father.

Little Tao was a spitting image of his mother. He was a bright, handsome lad about 4'6" tall and slender weighing about 85 lbs. He had a gap between his two top front teeth dutifully replicated by his mother's dominant genes within him. The boys in the school were split by age group and taught packets of Chinese wisdom and knowledge leaning on Confucius whenever his wisdom could emphasis a particular aspect of their training. Each child wore a red gi-like outfit with Chinese characters on their tops and sleeves that indicated their grade or position at the school equivalent to their academic level in a Western school. All boys were junior members of Ping's military force. They were initiated in Wu Shu early, and this training was continued all throughout their lives. Those that showed special abilities in math and science received advanced pace instruction in these disciplines.

Ping knew that the USA was the world leader and could only maintain that leadership as long as it had the military muscle to back it up. He wanted to nurture his own Einsteins to be first in the next level of weaponry. In this way, China could be the next number one world power with Ping as its emperor. Compared to Ping, American politicians and business executives who acted unethically in quest of large sums of privilege (money) looked like the angels who survived God's first cut.

Tao was also gifted with a moral sense of right and wrong. He knew that a lot of what he was being inculcated with was bullshit. He was a good kid and had a keen sense of justice. Tao knew just how far he could push his Chinese teachers and leaders before he got tossed off the railing. He was a lot smarter than they were; they thought that he had bought in to their inculcating agenda and would be an excellent scientist like his grandfather, Susan's father, who spent most of his life teaching chemistry at the university in Tianjin. Tao had his own program in mind, a daring escape into Nepal then on to America from Katmandu to be with his mother. So each day Tao listened to their Mandarin nonsense, nodding in agreement and behaving like a good little soldier. He knew and understood what they were making his mother do. He also surmised that even if she failed, it was unlikely that they would toss him into the valley because he had such great scientific potential. Ping might tell Susan that he was being beaten and would be tossed to get her cooperation, but it wasn't going to happen.

Nanchi, however, didn't have it so good. This daughter of Ling, junior librarian at Harrison College in Staten Island, was enrolled in the women's work-study program. This child abuse program continued the long legacy of subjugating women by the Chinese males. She had to get up at 4:00 a.m. to work in the kitchen to prepare the morning meal for the adults, mostly men, and for the other boys and girls held there. Nanchi was a very pretty true doll of America stationed China doll Ling. Ping would break her in himself when she turned thirteen, maybe sooner, and advance her to Hunan province for the next lot of China dolls set for the western United States.

5

THE SECOND DATE AND AFTERWARD—ROLLER SKATING

PUBLIC SKATE HOURS

SUNDAY	Public Skate	1PM - 4PM	$5 Admission	open October thru April
MONDAY	Public Skate	10AM - 1PM	$5 Admission	open October thru April
TUESDAY	Closed			
WEDNESDAY	Toddler Skate	12PM - 2PM	$3 Admission	7 yr. & under
	Public Skate	5PM - 8PM	$3 Admission	All Ages
		6PM - 8PM	$2 with Scout ID	*2nd Wednesday of every month
THURSDAY	Summer Skate	10AM - 2PM	$5 Admission	open end of June thru mid-August
FRIDAY	Public Skate	7PM - 10PM	$6 Admission	*3rd Fri. of every month - 70's/80's Mus
SATURDAY	Public Skate	7PM - 10PM	$6 Admission	Parents Skate Free with a paid child

During lunch at Linda's, Alex gathered certain key information that could be used to court Susan. He noticed that she used five sugars in her coffee, enough to feed Avogadro's number of ants for a microsecond. To gain favor with her, although this pathway wasn't clearly defined at this point in nurturing the relationship, he sent a bouquet of long-stem red roses to her at the restaurant (Chinese, of course) where she worked with the note, "To the Sweetest Girl in Town (five sugars, haha!); Alex." Using the word *love* seemed inappropriate at this time because he couldn't truthfully say that. If he was anything at all, he was in-your-face truthful to degrees that caused him grief. Once he daydreamed himself into an exact change lane on the GSP without exact change. He went through without paying but pulled over to the collectors' trailer offices to pay the quarter toll. No one in there could change a ten-dollar bill, and the counter person gave him a lecture on being in the right lane, etc. Alex swore that he would run the toll the next time after all the crap he received for a lousy quarter. However, he never ran a toll booth in his life—too honest and too much guilt and fear, not unusual for a Christian who was raised in the '50s.

Susan thanked him on the phone for the roses as she continued to call him every night of the week after their lunch date. Strange, he thought. *Why is this demure, apparently shy, soft-spoken girl calling me every night? Does she love me already? That would be great. It would be as if I had such personal magnetism and charm that women found me irresistible.* Girls did chase him all through his school years even in graduate school, but he avoided them like the plague for fear that his studies would suffer. Alex's brother's failure in college and his two older male first cousins' failures in college were due to heeding their Johnsons until Johnson made all the decisions. All Johnsons want action, not books, unless they're pornographic; a poor substitute for the real thing but better than nothing.

Girls chasing after boys are characteristic of aggressive women, not shy, demure ones. This inability to see the truth, temporarily blinded by infatuation coupled to his naivety with regard to women was soon to inflict great pain on Alex.

He arranges to go roller-skating with Sue on the following Saturday at a rink in Wayne. He had gleaned this information about her interests and hobbies at Linda's. Roller-skating wasn't something he liked to do, and it had been at least thirty years since he laced up a pair of these suckers. Susan already trusted him enough to have him pick her up near her apartment albeit on the corner, not at her entrance door.

He was driving his truck again because his '92 Honda Accord was being repaired. Someone had tried to steal it from his driveway, failed, and left three inches of a broken screw driver shank in the ignition. Although he worked it free, the damaged key tumblers failed to accept the true car key now. This would cost seven hundred fifty dollars to repair with an out-of-pocket cost of five hundred dollars due to the insurance company's deductible. This was a major intrusion into the shallow pockets of a poor chemist.

It's exactly 11:00 a.m. now. She is dressed in a black velvet overcoat with an embroidered silvery lace design on the shoulders and lapels. This gal seems to like velvet, and her taste is quite sophisticated and classy. After parking the truck on the nearby side street, Alex walks to greet her and hands her a single long-stem yellow rose. Taking her hand (throttling the groin nerve), he leads her to the warm light blue vinyl seat on the passenger side of his dark blue truck. She smiles pleasantly at him, and he nervously smiles back. He thinks that she looks 100 percent elegant and demure today and 0 percent sleazy. As she sits down in the truck, he notices she is wearing jeans under the overcoat. A light discussion ensues about the weather, the climate in China where she's from vs. the climate in this part of New Jersey. He tells her that she looks very pretty today, and she thanks him for the flowers that he sent but holds out the floral note card and asks, "What does this mean, 'Sweetest girl in town—five sugars'?"

"Oh, it's just something to make you laugh or smile. You used five bags of sugar in your coffee last week, so that makes you very sweet." She smiles again while dismissing his statement. She fails to appreciate his attempt at humor and drops the issue.

They arrive at the roller rink in Wayne next to a diner, park, and get in line as the facility wasn't yet fully opened. The zigzag line of people is mostly kids since Saturday is kid's day at the oval rink. As the cashier's window opens, Sue offers Alex some money for today's activity but is again rebuffed by her new and latest boyfriend. There were many, many other boyfriends before him. She has been excelling at her mission beyond Ping's wildest expectations. Ping wished that he had a thousand Susans before Alex wandered into her trap.

Alex rents the skates and pays the admission, and they proceed to a wall of small gray lockers. Here, Susan sheds her velvety overcoat while he sheds his brown leather bomber jacket and places his gently on top of hers in one of the small lockers after depositing two quarters to open it. He takes the locker key and pockets it. They lace up their four-wheel (black for him, white for her) rented skates, and Alex suddenly feels very unsure-footed and quickly falls on his buttocks. Susan helps him up, and they enter the ring holding hands for mutual support more than for love. His groin nerve pulsates wildly with her touch. *So far, so good*, he thinks silently. After two oval loops, Alex thinks that this is too much like hard work to be fun and rests along the dark stained side wood rail that encircles, um, en-ovals the rink. Susan is smiling and waving as she passes by on her nth trip around the oval. Finally, he reaches into his memory banks and remembers, more or less, how to roller skate. Alex catches up with his doll and grabs her hand gently, and they skate for a while as a couple. It is a satisfying sensation, and Alex very much would like to kiss Susan. She is so cool, sexy, and apparently vulnerable. He feels as if he should love and protect her. Alex is already falling in love with Susan. She seems to feel the same way by appearance, but in reality, she has detached herself from her emotions and is only doing her job.

Somehow Johnson has picked up on her detachment, remaining aloof and uninterested, hanging limp and flaccid. *Wake up, boy!* he intracommunicates. *Can't you see what I see? I want to have a hundred babies with this girl, a family, a sweet home, home on the range. This is the one! This is her, Johnson.* Johnson retreats into his foreskin like a turtle into its shell upon sensing danger. He senses trouble, danger, and pain. Johnson doesn't trust Susan, and Alex is baffled by it.

Showing off his newly returned skating skills, he rolls over to the snack counter and gets two Cokes then, with one Coke in each hand, very carefully glides over to Susan who is sitting at a rink side green Formica table.

"This is fun, isn't it?" he remarks with all the sincerity of an OPEC oil minister saying he is reducing oil prices.

Susan smiles showing those two separated top front teeth and says, "Yes, I like being here with you. Thank you for taking me and for the soda."

After about two hours, Alex feels every muscle in his legs cramping up and figures that if he doesn't get off these dumb skates soon, he may be unable to walk anymore, ever! He isn't twenty-eight anymore nor has he worked out lately at the karate dojo—it's been years. What you don't use, you can lose. Susan, God bless her, suggests that they leave and get something to eat. Staggering over to the lockers, he and Susan de-skate shoe (deplane?) and return the skates then leave the rink. They walk over to the neighboring Greek diner (is there another kind?) and draw the same quiet stares as they enter the ristorante.

The hostess inquires, "Two for lunch? Smoking or nonsmoking?"

"Nonsmoking please," states Alex. The couple is escorted to a booth in the far corner, and after perusing the menu, he, again upon Susan's request, orders for both of them.

"Two cheeseburger specials and two Cokes please," he says to the waitress. Lunch arrives, and Susan buries her french fries with nearly a half bottle of Heinz ketchup mimicking a scene out of the Texas chainsaw massacre. Alex contemplates, *Maybe ketchup is an expensive luxury in China, or maybe the color red is good luck for the Chinese*. This supposition of "good luck" turns out to be true. Chinese brides wear red at their wedding celebration. Alex would attend a Chinese wedding with Qing about six months after the breakup with Susan, i.e., six months after Susan dumped him and with extreme prejudice!

Small talk consumes another hour at the diner while Alex starts to think about having to get to work at 6:00 p.m. in Clark, NJ. They complete their lunch, then he helps Susan with her coat, pays the check, and escorts her back to his truck. While driving back to her apartment, Alex extends his right hand and cuddles Susan's left hand. She responds by holding his hand and gently rubbing her thumb back and forth over it. The thigh nerve begins to show life, and he is both pleased and mildly aroused by her gesture. Reaching her apartment, Susan demurely asks, "Would you like to come in for a little while?"

He is getting deeply into moral dilemma territory. He attempts to say, "No, thanks," but out of his mouth, to his surprise, comes, "Okay." They walk up the back staircase to her second-floor apartment, and Susan opens the doubly locked aged wooden door, enters, and is followed by Alex who is now in a conscious/semi-comatose state like a robot being controlled by this petite woman. The apartment is petite too, consisting of a 10'×12' kitchen dining room as you enter, a small half bath with a shower stall but sans a bathtub, a roughly 12×14' living room, bedroom, everything else room. The furniture is old, probably originating with the landlord in the form of a furnished apartment. Her kitchen table has only three chairs and her queen size bed is without a frame residing on the floor. There are photos of her parents and son, Tao, on the cheap parlor end tables but no ex-husband pictures. She has one picture of her standing with an older sister in China. The appearance difference is remarkable since her sister looks like a forty-ish preschool teacher compared to petite Susan's childlike, innocent look. Susan remarks that her older sister always referred to her as her little China doll, exactly the words that he has begun to refer to Susan.

Alex sits down at a table chair turned sideways and against the wall facing outward. Susan offers him something to drink, and he chooses orange juice, his staple drink in place of coffee. Another point in common surfaces in that neither consumes any alcohol at all, not even a beer. However, he glances at the refrigerator during her OJ retrieval and notices a six-pack of beer. *Who is that for?* he wonders. At a lull in the conversation and inspired by her readiness to draw circles on his hand during truck hand-holding, he pats his lap with his right hand without saying a word. To his complete shock, although by now the sleaze factor ratio to demure is at least a five, Susan, like a little puppy dog, obediently walks over to Alex and deposits herself directly onto his lap. They start to kiss, and Susan can really suck face, literally. She uses an open mouth vacuum to keep her mouth tightly adhered to his. He is really enjoying himself now, but Johnson is totally immobilized as the sleaze factor ratio now exceeds ten. This has got to be the sexiest kissing he ever experienced even though the tongue has yet to enter the picture. Little miss dangerous and Alex continues petting for about twenty minutes when he suddenly exclaims out of the blue, "Well, I have to go to work now. It will be late when I get home from work, so I'll call you tomorrow, okay?"

"Okay," Susan answers softly but obviously aroused and frustrated. "I wish you could stay longer."

"Me too," he says, but he is really becoming frightened by the aggressiveness of this pretty woman. It seems to be surfacing in little ways through myriad events. He has been with her a total of about eight hours, and she is already kissing with her mouth open and obviously wants more. She is hot, too hot at this point in their budding relationship. The sleaze factor ratio is up an order of magnitude and stands at one hundred. But Alex is dangerously inquisitive and drawn to her to pursue the relationship in spite of all the red flags surfacing in his consciousness.

He departs with one last goodbye kiss, and her tongue with the suction now comes into play. A normal man would have wet his pants due to her extremely sexual kissing. As it is, Alex staggers weakly down the back staircase to his truck with a near attack of panic though dangerously excited. Mr. Rationalization begins to lecture him. *Maybe she just wants to show me that she likes me a lot and wants to encourage me to keep dating her. Maybe it's the Chinese way with women. Maybe, maybe…maybe…definitely maybe she's a little whore. Maybe she's the best thing that's ever happened to me. Slow down, slooooooooow down, boy, we're moving much too fast. Johnson, what do you think?*

Johnson is asleep and hiding—he is terrified. Johnson then relates, *I do not want to be in this woman. There's something very wrong with her. I'm going into the situational ED mode until you know her better. However, for both our safety, I advise you to split from this relationship.*

What's this? Alex is willing but Johnson isn't? The tables are reversed. For other men, their Johnsons would be saying, "Go, man, go!" while his owner would say, "Be careful, but go, man, go!" They would let their Johnsons make their decisions for them in sex matters, and Johnson is usually proactive with any female with the required characteristics, a pussy and a heartbeat.

Alex continues to ruminate as he drives down the GSP toward work in Clark on Terminal Road. Terminal? Terminated is what this relationship should be. What kind of wife/mother can she be if she's so promiscuous? *If she's this easy with me, how many men has she been with? Maybe she's diseased by now. Stop it! Damn it. All she did was kiss you very affectionately. There was no sex…yet. "I did not have sex with that woman," to quote our fearless leader.*

Regroup and proceed with a little caution. Let's not deep-six this relationship yet. She still is very pretty and desirable. Remember, you have a fail-safe to protect you. Besides, wasn't it you who patted your lap, suggested the deluge of romantic, um, semi-sexual activities?

So he decides to continue with Susan because it's dangerously exciting. This is new experiential turf for him with no precedent to follow.

He parks his truck in the company lot on Terminal Road and card-keys the building entrance. His technician is happy to see him because now she can go home. They trade places, and he is now at work and alone with his thoughts of the day with Susan.

6

ALEX'S MORAL/MORALE DILEMMA

Okay, Johnson, we need to have a long talk so that I can whip you into the proper moral perspective while still maintaining "our" morale. As you probably recall, you first saw action when thirty-seven years old (virgin till then). Why not sooner? It was because you were guided by the moral codes of the church. Then, one look at Susan and the church went out the window. Didn't you once speculate that if you had a chance at refusing Eve's apple, you could pass the test and all of mankind could still be in paradise? If Susan were Eve and she offered, i.e., was willing, initiated some action of the horizontal variety, could you resist? I don't think so,

Johnson, despite your cavalier attitude at the roller rink. Luckily and simultaneously unluckily, we have a fail-safe mechanism. Situational impotency, aka ED.

Luckily? Johnson beams loudly. He continues, *We had to forego at least one hundred offers from thirty or more different women over the last twenty-seven years. There I was, ready to go, but then after thirty minutes of foreplay with no progression toward "doing it," I would start to lose interest. After the first several times, I remained interested for at least those thirty minutes, but after ten different desirable women with no action, I gave up. Now I don't even bother to get up to salute. Why should I? You're going to listen to your overbearing conscience, be a nice guy, and I get nothing. What's in it for me? Sometimes being a nice guy is not working up the girl to willingness, then cutting her off—that's painful for her emotionally and physically. Remember the case of "blue balls" that you experienced when you were fifteen? Sometimes, especially with women of low self-esteem, being a nice guy means giving her what she wants. It's a greater "sin"* (error) *not having intercourse with her, leaving her all wet and frustrated.*

They'll be no *standing* ovation for a great performance in the flaccid state because there is no such thing. *What are you going to do, liquefy me and pour me inside her? It commits us to commitment, and we need a girl with patience and understanding and, most of all, a low sex drive. So regardless of thoughts of being a stud with Susan, the relationship's progression to doing it will be as slow as a green box turtle crawling across the black top on a hot and arid day. She'll have to marry us before she gets any, and then maybe.*

"What the hell is this? My penis is talking to me?"

As Alex and Johnson ruminate over these philosophical considerations concerning God, sex, the church, ED, etc., Susan has a program of her own to destroy this professional American male. After all, it is the girl who controls the sexual progress of a relationship. The guy goes for it and either gets it or gets beaten back physically, psychologically, or morally, retreating from the scene with both him and his Johnson feeling flaccid in more ways than one. Alex's morality is automatically asserting itself in this arena, and strangely, this will save his life. From the little intelligence gathered thus far, Susan could go either way; she could be a saint or a whore being still demure yet sleazy, although the close encounter at her apartment after the skating date definitely stacks the deck in the whore direction. Alex was an extremist and usually failed to see a middle route.

Heck, maybe she's a virgin! Yeah, right, she got her nine-year-old son by artificial insemination—fat chance, especially in the land of the permanent hard-on, China.

Here's the plan: go slow, don't push the sex thing, and play it by ear. After each close encounter of the third kind, regroup and reevaluate then adjust your behavior accordingly. In the unlikely event that she is a whore, split. No social diseases for us, thank you. Hold emotions at bay until you see that she will commit to you demonstrating the qualities of patience, understanding, and love. Get her to say "I love you" (Wo ai ni) and agree to cooperate in curing your problem ED before getting emotionally involved.

There is a delicate balance required here like that of a gymnast on the 11/2-inch balance beam. We must keep our morals intact simultaneously with keeping our morale intact. Unfortunately, one seems to work against the other. Morale will be up with Johnson up, but morals will keep Johnson at bay, flaccid, enhancing morality but obliterating morale-ity. This is too complicated. Why can't I just get laid like every other American guy? Sometimes, in fact, most times I curse my impotency and would rather have experienced regular sexual activity development so that I could act on instinct. These are the makings of a classic neurosis—pursuing something and being blocked from attaining it.

We'll see how it goes with this gal. It might even work out.

But unbeknownst to Alex, Sue's plan for him is very short term, and he is really chasing his own tail like Ouroboros, the mythological asp. Soon, very soon, he will experience a very hard lesson, but not in his pants.

7

WU SHU CAMP: KOWLOON BAY AREA, HONG KONG

To ensure that the job would get done if the China dolls failed, each doll was assigned a jealous ex-husband who was well trained in the Chinese martial arts, wushu (aka kung fu). These men were the elite of the Chinese culture, revered like the Shaolin priests once were. In the USA, the closest branch of the fighting services that resembled these wushu warriors were the Navy SEALS or the Vietnam era Green Berets. Deng Zhao Ping wanted them to be his own special "ninja" (assassins) force, capable of using ancient as well as conventional weapons including their bodies to kill on command then blend into the scenery incapable of being found. Using special surreptitious tactics, these killers would essentially disappear. Each SPS agent had several "ex-wives" in America that he was responsible for. They would report to Ping weekly concerning the success or failure of each of their charges.

Although the SPS were extensively trained in kung fu along with the non-humane practical aspects of Buddhism like meditative and concentration (focus) techniques, Ping had greatly overestimated their abilities and loyalty to his conspiracy. They could easily take out two or three strapping defensive linemen of a pro football team with their speed and techniques. However, they were no match for the hard forms of karate and ninjutsu taught in American dojos where an individual was free to choose his physical training regimen and the level of intensity with which he or she pursued it. In hand-to-hand kumite (sparring, fighting) using legs and other parts of the body (but no weapons), a single disciplined, ardent American practitioner or Navy SEAL could kick three of their asses at once without breaking a sweat. The average SEAL was about 6'1", 185 pounds of well-conditioned body and mind, whereas the average Chinese warrior was 5'6" at 140 pounds. The SEALS' code of honor and brotherhood made the SPS look like mercenaries who were ready to run if they couldn't handle the situation. Chairman Ping overrated his men and greatly underrated the American warriors because he thought that they lacked discipline due to the morally decadent society of the United States.

Ping's second mistake was to choose Kowloon, just across the bay from Hong Kong, for the location of his training camps. He didn't realize that this area was too westernized to sustain the rigid discipline required of true martial artists. Deng (pronounced "dung" appropriately) thought that this location would be ideal because he wanted to have his "ex-husbands" acclimatized to Western influences and culture so that they would blend better and not become readily susceptible to the worst elements of a free market society.

Elements like drugs, alcohol, prostitution, and other cheap thrills or good times might cause defections into the otherwise desirable American way of life albeit novel to his men. The plan backfired on him since many of his agents were initiated to or already strung out on one drug or another during their training in Kowloon. Sex was a totally acceptable drug in China since virtually everything else was banned. It was the logical choice for the Chinese culture, which had been using women and killing female babies for centuries.

In spite of these handicaps, his agents were still a formidable killing squad, just not as formidable as they should have been.

Alex's training started right before Vietnam and continued there as he was prepared to serve in a Marine recon division. On his second tour, he was a field artillery commander near the DMZ. But before and after the war ended, he had been researching and studying physical chemistry in the daytime and practicing a hard form of karate every night. As a black belt, he had his own key to the dojo and would frequently be found there on Thursday and Sunday mornings too. The Thursday morning class comprised mostly black belts with flexible work/study schedules like his graduate school research or like cops who alternated working three shifts. This is where he became friends with Sensei Thomas, a sixth degree black belt with the correct philosophy for a true martial arts instructor. Sensei Thomas believed in the inner strength and value of a humble man like many eastern philosophies advocated. This was in stark contrast to most American dojos where the instructor encouraged big egos in his black belts using it almost as an incentive for them to study karate. Alex first approached Sensei Thomas's dojo to train in karate because he hated fighting and wanted to have the inner strength to walk away from a potential fight like Caine in the TV series *Kung Fu*. Thomas's dojo gave him exactly what he wanted; he didn't pick fights to see how tough he was but acted quickly and firmly once a punch was thrown at him to evade it and end the fight with one or two blows. He wasn't alone with this attitude at Sensei Thomas's training center in Hawthorne, NJ. There were many like him, i.e., weak and nerdy-looking in appearance but tough sons of a sea cook when it was necessary to fight. Most of their real street fights lasted a few seconds with their loudmouth, macho opponents hitting the tar with a broken rib or two, or a cracked jaw. Sparring, technique, and kata practicing were for the dojo; ending the fight quickly was for the street.

Alex made many friends there, people that he could and would count on to help him later in life. He also developed an interest in

Okinawan weapons training after he became a second degree black belt. This interest in weapons extended itself into 9 mm Berettas in a police pistol club that many of his cop friends were members of. These skills coupled strangely to his lack of skill in lovemaking, viz ED, were to serve him well once he stumbled upon Susan and Ping's termination program.

Back in Kowloon, the Chinese men were lined up according to rank in the musty, dingy training hall which was dimly lit and frequently blacked out entirely; Ping wasn't always on time paying the electric bill—damn these capitalistic societies that he had no direct control over. Tao, Susan's "ex-husband," was really her estranged husband. In China, women were finally given the right to divorce their husbands, and they did so in droves. Just about every Chinese girl from the mainland that Alex met was divorced. Of course a Chinese divorce didn't restrict the rights of the ex-husbands to drop in unexpectedly for sex (aka rape) whenever they couldn't find someone else. The courts in the mainland were staffed with only male judges who wouldn't even hear a case of a woman who was "raped" by her ex. There was no such thing as a female being raped in China; she usually "asked for it" by her appearance or behavior.

Tao was a high-ranking SPS and lead the training frequently. Today was endurance training. This is where Tao gets to throw a trainee's female concubine into the middle of the bay to see if that trainee can rescue her and bring her back to land. This was a mere swimming lesson under duress of about one-fourth of a mile. Once in a while one of his warriors would succeed. Most of the time the warrior would get only himself back to shore, thus having to find a new concubine. Occasionally a warrior would drown. "There were too many people in China anyway, especially women," Tao would say. Kind of killing two birds with one stone: reducing the population while weeding out the weaklings from his killing force. It didn't really matter what Tao thought or said since he was following a direct order given to him personally by Chairman Ping. Disobedience meant Tao would become, well, dead rather painfully and slowly.

Some other aspects of the SPS agents training were similar to the SEALS. For example, the maneuvering across and into the line of gunfire was practiced. The Chinese version used real bullets and any straddlers would join intimately with one of those bullets launched at him from Ping's marksmen, resulting in acute lead poisoning.

On the other hand, the rewards for success in training and in America were great. For each successful kill, an agent would get ten credits. When he reached a certain number of credits, he could cash them in on "prizes." One of the prizes was a weekend of liberty in one of America's red light districts with enough cash, drugs, or whatever he needed to secure the services of big-breasted American whores for seventy-two full hours. Another prize that required a large number of credits was an all-expense paid trip back to the mainland so that an agent could verify that his wife and family were still alive and spend a few days with them. The fear that Ping had of defection was so great that even Chinese scholars sent to the USA to study for advanced degrees were not allowed to bring their wives or children with them; their families retained in China served as an insurance policy against defections to the free world.

Opium was always the preferred drug in Chinese territories, and it was also dispensed as a reward for meritorious work in the US for very few credits. Ping liked opium both as a drug that he took and as a means to control his agents. Once addicted to opium, an agent would do surprising things to keep his supply coming. Bold, exciting things like daylight assassinations in New York City to make death count quotas. Previously well-disciplined and low-keyed agents became dangerously bold to do anything rather than face withdrawal symptoms.

Tao, Susan's ex-husband and mentor, was a natural leader who was also, unfortunately, the first to get hooked on crack, a white piece of soap like ice that Ping didn't deal in because there was too much competition. Tao could exhibit the strength of three men when up on crack. Alex, on the other hand, had to take a tricyclic antidepressant to keep his panic disorder under control. This drug made him invulnerable to cocaine and its derivatives because it blocked the uptake of coke by those brain centers, the synaptic nerve endings that cocaine locked onto to produce its euphoric effect. High spirits, overestimation of one's abilities, and, most dangerously, a feeling of confidence that ensured the user that he could take it or leave it and was in full control of his cravings were the properties of cocaine. This was the devil's own best drug in his arsenal which he used to cause the downfall of men. Unfortunately, after the high comes the crash, which was very much like a panic attack; hence, the junkies' desperate, mad search for more coke immediately killed many individuals during their unlawful pursuits to attain this goal.

Tao, in pursuit of more crack, once stealthily broke into Malcolm Sharks' warehouse in Harlem, the local distribution center amidst the half demolished tenements and empty lots strewn with garbage and drug paraphernalia. To his surprise, Sharks was there and didn't waste any time trying to blow him away with his German Sig Sauer 9 mm. Fortunately for Tao, the gun jammed, and Tao was able to disable the two guards at the backdoor with his keen knowledge of wushu. To Sharks, all chinamen looked alike, so Tao blended back into the sea of Chinatown never to be seen by Sharks' runners again. Tao knew not to go anywhere near there after the first encounter for fear of his life. Sharks had a reputation to uphold.

Alex would find Tao a formidable opponent, especially when the latter was spaced out on something. His advantage, though, would be clear, analytical way of thinking and his quick reaction time to imminent physical threats; Sensei Thomas used to allow only Alex to do a practice technique for speed that Sensei did as a demonstration for karate shows. He would stand about twenty-five feet from an archer who would launch an arrow at him on a three count, and Alex would catch or deflect the arrow rendering it harmless. This was not a technique that most black belts even dared to try let alone succeed at. Another advantage for him was that Tao didn't know that cocaine had no effect on him. Even if Alex got captured or trapped by a few Tao's associates and they injected him or forced him to snort coke, he could fake the high while brewing up an escape path as they dropped their guard like Nicola Toscani did in the kitchen scene in *Above the Law*.

Tao was busy booking a flight to JFK from Kowloon Bay to meet Alex then to Staten Island to terminate an American professor of English who got infected by Ling, the doctorate intellectual China doll. Dr. Clifford Jude figured out that Ling didn't really love him and refused to quietly disappear. After dispatching Alex, Tao would go to a small college in Staten Island where Ling was assigned to finish what she had begun. Dr. Jude was in the process of greatly damaging Ping's conspiracy, so Tao had to act fast before Ping found out from some other SPS agents.

8

SEDUCTIVE ENCOUNTERS OF THE TONGUE KIND—THE THIRD DATE

The weeknights after date two are again occupied in part by Susan's nightly phone calls. Somehow Alex and her find something to talk about for nearly an hour each night. Still sounding like a demure little girl, Alex has seen a different Susan from the one he is listening to. They make plans to go ice-skating at Bear Mountain, New York, on the soon arriving Saturday. Bear Mountain occupies a special place in Alex's heart since he used to go there yearly on a school trip with Mom by Hudson River Day Liner from NYC when it took three hours to get there. There's a small zoo and wildlife center, a Swiss chalet for eating and rooming, bars, and large open areas leading to Hessian Lake. Averell Harriman donated most of the land so that

(NY) city people could have a rural, country spot to picnic and relax. Knowing its ins and outs, Alex feels safe there.

The Saturday arrives, and he goes to pick up his date at her second-floor apartment in Nutley. She is dressed neatly with a pair of pleated beige slacks and a white blouse buttoned to the neck. It completely conceals whatever she has for breasts as they barely lift the blouse from her chest.

While driving up Route 17 toward Bear Mountain, Susan is holding Alex's gear-shifting right hand with both her hands placing it on her lap. This is just a few tenths of an inch of clothing and a couple of inches of space from her essence. The twitchy groin area nerve clicks into action like a six-year-old with a new Nintendo game. Johnson is freaking and assuming his turtle configuration. At that moment, Alex is distracted by a gray Nissan Sentra, just like Susan's, that seems to be following them. He gets off Route 17 onto Seven Lakes Drive and makes a tire-squealing quick left turn parking the truck behind a delicatessen. He tells Susan that he wants to get a Coke and he'll be right back. Peering out the store window, he sees the Nissan continue past the store going east on Seven Lakes Drive toward Bear Mountain. Alex gets his Coke and returns to the truck. Smiling at Susan, he starts the engine and continues up Seven Lakes Drive thinking that he is getting a little paranoid due to the nervous excitement of being with Sue.

They finally arrive at the outdoor rink about 11:00 a.m. Alex gets a black pair of figure skates for himself and a borrowed white pair for Susan from the back of the truck under the cap. He trades his blue overcoat for a tighter fitting down jacket. Sue remarks, "You look completely different in that jacket." Alex laughs and escorts his date to the admission line. He pays the fees, and the couple enters the ice rink hand in hand.

After about forty-five minutes of skating ovals, Alex is resting on the side rail as Susan zips by smiling at him and egging him on. Quickly tiring of this activity, it seems like a good time for lunch. The couple leaves the rink and drive to the Chalet. After paying the four-dollar parking fee, they walk holding hands to the restaurant. Susan can't wait to get her french fries and quickly drowns them with half of a bottle of ketchup. Alex pays the check as they deduct four dollars for the parking fee (eat lunch, park free is standard policy) but leaves another four dollars as a generous tip. He and Susan leave the building and walk toward the truck when Alex spots the gray Nissan Sentra again, being driven by an oriental guy. They get into the truck and proceed up the mountain to the Perkins Drive overlook. Parking on the backside of the mountain, Alex gets out and assists Susan in her step down to the ground from the 4WD vehicle. From this point, you can see Hessian Lake, the lodge, the Hudson River, and the surrounding mountains—it's a beautiful view from an elevation of about two thousand feet. No one else is on this side of the mountain at this time when the gray Nissan pulls up and parks about ten feet from the couple. A short muscular oriental guy gets out of the car and walks right toward Alex and Susan. He stops about five feet away and speaks something that sounds like Chinese.

"What's he want, Susan?" remarks Alex.

She says, "He wants to know why a pretty Chinese girl like me is holding hands with an American pig. He says that I am a disgrace to mother China."

Alex, sensing imminent danger, tells Susan to warn him off. He says, "Tell him I am a second degree black belt in karate (wushu), and we don't want any trouble, so we're leaving."

Susan translates, but the stocky fellow just laughs and positions himself between the truck and the couple. Alex walks first with Susan following and attempts to avoid a confrontation by cutting a wide arc around this nut to return to his truck. Suddenly a knife appears, and the stocky Chinese charges toward Alex. Instinctively, Alex waits until the very last moment, sidesteps the attacker then grabs his arm, and redirects his attacking momentum planting a back kick in the small of his back and propelling him off the cliff into some trees about ten feet below.

"C'mon, Susan, let's get out of here before he wakes up." The couple gets into the truck and quickly descends the mountain toward Route 17.

Susan is silently thinking, *Why did they send Tao already? Can't they wait another week?*

Alex is also silent and a little shook up. He thinks to himself, *Am I back in Vietnam in a Saigon bar again? This is America. Things like knifings don't happen on Perkins' overlook.* Then he asks Susan point-blank, "Do you know that guy?"

Susan is now perspiring even though it's mid-winter. She says, "He is crazy lunatic. I have never seen him before," continuing the chain of lies which began with their first phone call. Silence ensues.

Alex, in the excitement and terror of the moment, forgot to copy the license plate number which he could check against Susan's. After all, how many four-door gray '92 Nissan Sentra can there be within a fifty-mile radius? Then, he softens his thinking and stops believing that Susan and this guy are associated in some way. How could they be? She's so sweet and affectionate. *Too affectionate*, chimes in Johnson.

The trip back to Susan's apartment is without further incident, peaceful, and calm, more or less. When they reach the corner where Sue was picked up, she asks, "Would you like to come in for a soda or something?"

Something? thinks Alex. *I wonder what that includes.*

Coffee, tea, or me, suggests Johnson.

Shut up, Johnson, Alex speaks silently. The exciting feeling of danger magnified by the knife attack pulls Alex into her apartment, again. As he enters slowly, he is half expecting a samurai to jump out and slash off his head. No one is there; the apartment is empty as the couple walks in. *Samurai, shamurai—they're Japanese anyway*, Alex thinks, busting his own chops.

After some orange juice and small talk, Susan comes over to Alex and sits on his lap uninvited. Alex has no valid reason this weekend why he must leave early and becomes very tense. Susan initiates the foreplay with a small kiss on his lips. "What beautiful blue eyes you have," she says, sounding almost sincere.

"What beautiful, exotic black eyes you have," returns Alex. Then, spontaneously, the couple begins to kiss deeply, and Susan applies an open-mouth vacuum simultaneously lurching her tongue deeply into his mouth. She is telling him that she wants more; she wants him, today, now. Johnson is unmoved and unmotivated despite the intense flavor of her French kisses that would cause any other man to soil himself instantly. Alex is very scared and convinced that he may not be able to "perform." So after working her up to a fever pitch, he says, "I love you." Big mistake. Susan looks at him queerly, smiles, and goes back to trying to give him a tonsillectomy with her suction and tongue kisses. *This is worse than Chinese water torture,* Alex is thinking. *She wants me inside her, and I can't get Johnson to cooperate. I have to get out of here before she sees that I can't perform.*

Alex mumbles something about a lot of work he needs to do at home to her and makes a hasty retreat. Susan says, "Why don't you stay here?" meaning sleep with her. Alex, wishing he were nineteen again, stands up as she leaves his lap. He puts on his blue coat with the gray faux fur collar, and she comes to him. She embraces him tightly, and Alex can feel the strength of this little woman. Then she kisses him with her special formula nearly knocking his socks off. He exits quickly, while he still can, down the back staircase and across the street to his waiting truck.

During the forty-five minutes it takes to drive home, Alex is reassessing his relationship with Sue. The sleaze factor just went up two orders of magnitude. *Could this be the way with all Chinese women?* he contemplates. Knowing that he must end this relationship but feeling excited about the possibility of sex with her, Alex is torn and indecisive. He wants to, but all the red flags point to no. Johnson, meanwhile, is so far buried in his foreskin that he is nearly invisible.

Alex turns left onto his dirt road home street then drives the truck up his long rocky driveway.

I won't call her tonight. I've got to clear my head and act rationally, do what's right, safe. Maybe I should buy some condoms just in case.

In case of what? Johnson interjects. *Alex, wake up, boy! There is no way I'm going to cooperate with you re Susan Long. We will be hurt, and I won't let that happen. I'm locked in the fail-safe mode.*

Again, Alex tells Johnson to shut up and stop confusing him. He'll do what he wants to, and Johnson will have to just go along with his decision, get with the program. Besides, who's the boss here anyway? Who makes the decisions? Johnson has been silenced for the moment knowing he has the final say.

9

STEALTH OF AN SPS AGENT: TAO VISITS STATEN ISLAND

As Tao pulled up to the guard house checkpoint at Harrison College, he handed the aged, nearly blind former police officer a fake ID from SUNY Binghamton and told him that he was here to present a seminar in the history department, using the name of the current Harrison department of history's chairperson, Dr. Silvia Benson, as a reference. The old guard casually looked at the ID and waved him through. Tao parked the gray Nissan by a guest post in a lot that overlooks the Verrazano Narrows Bridge to Brooklyn.

He reaches under the front seat and pulls out a Glock 9 mm and silencer unattached. From the glove compartment, he picks out his favorite knife, a Chinese replica of a bowie, and places it in its sheath then puts it in a deep side pocket of his sport coat. The Glock goes under his belt near the small of his back, something he learned from watching American detective movies. One way or the other, Cliff Jude taught his last class today on the tree-covered campus of Harrison College.

Seminar times run at 4:30 p.m. when most faculty, staff, and students have already left for the day. There was no night or graduate school at Harrison, so the campus was fairly desolate. It was a cloudy, overcast day with the smell of snow in the air; since Tao arrived, it had already started to get dark. Now there was the smell of death in the air too.

The campus was a compact fifty acres, so one could walk from one end to the other in about seven minutes. The English department occupied the second floor in Jamieson Hall, named after the first professor of English who was awarded a Pulitzer Prize in literature.

Tao is walking casually on the ten-foot wide tar path toward Jamieson Hall. Being one of the oldest buildings on campus, it was donated by the Harrison family with the fifty acres in 1907 to the city of New York, borough of Staten Island. It was a pre-Spanish American war mansion three stories high made of red brick, has thirty-seven windows and four entrance doors, one for each geographical direction. Tao entered the building from the west on the ground floor through a marble arched doorway. Dressed in a dark blue blazer and khaki pants and wearing round glasses, he looked like any other professor on campus carrying a dark brown briefcase. This briefcase contained validity establishing props viz: a stack of fictitious test papers from a supposed recently given exam and a textbook of the history of the Chinese people in America. Tao goes directly to the black directory board hanging on the beige wall at the main entrance and looks for Dr. Jude's office number. *Room 214, second floor directly above me*, he thinks to himself. As Tao walks up the staircase, he can smell the heat rising in the old mansion. Its odor is a blend of old books with a slight diesel smell produced by the sixty-year-old oil burner still in service located in the basement. It is unusually hot in the stairwell. At the second-floor landing, double doors guard the entrance to the offices. Tao pushes them open and proceeds to walk in the wrong direction away from room 214. As he is walking, he inadvertently drops his car keys that he has been nervously jingling in his hand since he left the Nissan. Professor Jude hears the echoing jangle of the keys hitting the floor and steps out of his office to see what caused the noise. Tao bends over to pick up his keys unknowingly exposing the Glock 9 mm stuffed into his belt. Jude becomes immediately alarmed, goes back into his office, and slams and locks the door. The glass in the door vibrates madly, almost shattering. Tao, hearing the door slam and realizing that he has been walking the wrong way, sprints towards room 214. Jude is on the phone trying to raise security, but the line is busy. Tao gets to the door, tries it, but it is locked. He can see the shadow of someone in the room whom he assumes is Dr. Jude. Looking both ways and seeing no one, Tao smashes the window on the door, reaches through, and unlocks the door. As he walks in, a loaded bookcase of English literature books comes crashing down on top of him. Cursing in Mandarin but undismayed, he gets up and goes to an interior door. It is locked, but the door has no window in it. He grabs the phone cord and rips it out of the wall socket. Then, approaching the locked lauan door, he steps forward and gives it a good front kick. His foot goes through the door, but the lock holds. Reaching through the hole, Tao begins to unlock the door when he feels intense pain in his left arm. Jude has stabbed him with a pair of scissors that are still in his arm as he retracts it through the hole in the door. Tao is maniacally angry at this point. He repeatedly kicks the lauan door until the lock finally gives out. Opening the door carefully, he enters the interior room as Dr. Jude is pummeling him with anything he can get his hands on. Tao gets hit smack-dab right on the forehead with a stapler, which he picks up and throws back at Jude hitting him in the chest and knocking the wind out of him temporarily. Cursing in Chinese, he next endures an armchair to the legs slid on its wheels toward him by the resilient professor. Jude has now run out of projectiles to launch at Tao and stands motionless in the office screaming at the top of his lungs. "Help! Someone help me!"

Tao has reached the limit of his patience, which, for him, isn't a long journey. He reaches back and pulls out his Glock 9 mm, screws on the silencer, and says, "This is for you, Dr. Jude," then fires two rounds into him. "The next two are for screwing up my arm, you American pig!" Tao says as he pumps two more rounds into him. "These last two are for giving me such a hard time. Die, you big deal professor," says Tao as he pulls the trigger of the semi-automatic two more times. *Pfuuf, pfuuf.* Jude drops like a rock across the desk quite dead.

There is a commotion in the hallway at this point as others have been reviled by Jude's screaming. Tao calmly takes a rope out of a secret compartment in his briefcase, cuts off a small piece with the scissors, and secures a tourniquet to his left forearm. Then he opens the window and, using his knife, stuck deeply into the top of a wooden desk as a pivot point, secures the rope to it. He goes out the window and rappels down the back wall of Jamieson Hall to a grassy mound below the window. He casually walks through the tree-studded campus back to his car under the cover of darkness as campus security and the local police enter Jude's outer office with guns drawn and fixed in both hands. Slowly, covering themselves with each step, they enter the interior room. It is in shambles with office supplies and books all over the floor, blood splattered on the walls and ceiling with the late professor lying across his desk face down as if he were studying the pattern of the floor tiles. One officer checks his neck in the hope of finding a pulse. Nothing. Professor Jude has been forcibly retired.

Curiosity assembles a small group of people, which a second police officer disperses as he begins to seal off the crime scene. The other officer radios headquarters on his handset and requests a medical examiner.

Meanwhile, Tao has already left the campus nodding to the security guard on his way out. He is heading for the Verrazano Bridge then over the Brooklyn Bridge back to the Chinatown headquarters to file his report with Ping. He will be pleased—this is an extra twenty credits for Tao to pocket. Eliminating a full-fledged professor rids Ping of one of the leaders of free thinking who can impede his program by using logic. If it were a science professor, it would be fifty extra credits because these people are the ones ultimately responsible for America's world leadership. Sports, movies, and rock concerts may generate large amounts of money but add nothing to the security of a nation. The key is the scientists; their work leads to better weaponry, and superior weaponry leads to world domination in the hands of the right person—Ping.

10

THE CHINA DOLL HEADQUARTERS IN CHINATOWN

Tao gets into Chinatown at about 7:00 p.m. due to the heavy working class traffic going to and from Staten Island. He drives to the SoHo municipal parking lot up to level three and parks the Nissan. Instead of hailing a cab, he walks the several congested blocks to Bayard St. so as not to arouse suspicion as he cradles his left arm in a makeshift sling covered with blood under his coat. Below Ming's beauty parlor, there is a coded entrance to Ping's computer works network. Punching in the access code on the door lock, he steps inside and proceeds to the door at the back of the computer room. The room has a low ceiling of about six feet, but most Chinese have several inches of clearance to the dirty, tin and tan ceiling while many

Westerners would need to bend to negotiate the room. Tao opens the rear door and sits down on a high hospital-like table as a Chinese herbal doctor comes to him to treat and bandage his arm. Dr. Wang is a certified acupuncturist and herbalist. Combining a mixture of ground deer antlers with some dried scorpion tail and chamomile, he applies it to Tao's arm, and the bleeding stops immediately. Wang then bandages the arm and puts it in a proper prosthetic-looking sling. No arteries have been severed despite the depth of the gash. One inch to the right and Tao would be sacrificing that arm up to the elbow as if it were severely frostbitten on Mount Everest. Wang gives Tao a little opium to ease the throbbing pain, and moments later, he is relaxing on the table in a prone position. He falls asleep but is rudely awakened by a ruckus in the computer room. Apparently some NY police are asking questions about a murder that occurred earlier in Staten Island. The cops are ethnic Chinese and are speaking Cantonese dialect in this part of Chinatown. Of course, nobody knows anything. One of the policemen asks, "What's behind that door?" At that prompting, the doctor and Tao disappear into a secret tunnel that leads to the street about a block uptown. The cops get the door open to find the room completely empty. Just a high table and some chairs, and the smell of phenol fills the room. They fail to consider and thus do not locate the secret tunnel. Curiosity satisfied, they leave the computer complex and file their report. No sign of anyone suspicious, area clean.

Tao has decided to not go back there to file his report to Ping. He can do it from his apartment on Canal Street. Back at the garage, he retrieves his car and drives to his apartment, a three-story pre-WW I brick building. The dingy, dark alleyway between this building and the next serves as a parking space, a real premium in a city of eight million people.

After opening the triply latched door, Tao walks in and boots up his Microwest computer—Ping was never into brand names for his workers; generics was what his country made.

The computer prompts Tao for the following:

User:
Access Code:
Password:

Tao types in:

Tao Chen
666
China doll

In Beijing, the small camera on Ping's computer comes to life showing him sitting in his office. When he sees it automatically boot up, he walks over to the keyboard and sits down. His office has mahogany paneled walls with a red Persian carpet displaying the Chinese flag with Ping's name in kanji. His desk is solid cherry wood imported from Montana's Glacier National Park. The computer station is dark walnut laminated pine straight from an IKEA showroom in Hicksville, LI. Ping has surrounded himself with all the American trappings to help him keep focused on his goal, emperor of the USA. The only hint of China in his furniture is his emperor's chair behind the cherry wood desk. It is heavily cushioned to ease Ping's hemorrhoids caused by sitting on his ass too much and delegating. The wood is adorned with typical excesses of red, gold, and green. It was hand carved by skilled Thai woodcrafters in Bangkok.

Ping sees Tao's tired face and is pleased because of an advanced report he received from Tao's overseers. Every person working in the conspiracy had at least one other person watching him. The fax said that SI intellectual target CJ has been successfully retired with no apprehension of the principal operative.

Tao speaks into the microphone near his photo-optic. "Honorable, exalted Chairman Ping. Today is a great day for the future of China." Tao gets carried away into excesses due to his crack habit. "CJ of SI intellectual target retired, apprehension avoided. Next target AS of NJ, PhD. Physical chemist. He is skilled in wushu—will require two additional SPS agents preferably skilled in karate styles. One associate attack on ASNJ resulted in serious injuries to associate. Also, agents should be 9 mm-qualified sharpshooters. May need to snipe from a distance if resistance is heavy when attempt is made in Virginia this weekend. Thank you, honorable, exalted Chairman Ping, for this opportunity to serve you and Motherland China."

Ping is pleased indeed. Tao will get thirty extra credits for CJSI. Ping further entices Tao to retire ASNJ by upping the extra credits to one hundred from fifty, a sort of combat pay. Ping signs off as his Russian concubine enters naked for his massage. Ping is tickled pink, or is that red? Natasha starts the massage at his crotch. Ping is getting excited and lies back on his office couch, a red-and-gold print from Huffman-Koos, and prepares to enjoy himself. He thinks to himself, *Stupid Americans, they believe that God will save them from everything. Tao just proved there is no God to help when Ping is determined to succeed.* This Nietzsche restatement will prove to be the main downfall of Ping's brilliant conspiracy.

11

THE ULTIMATE HUMILIATION BUT SALVATION

As usual, Alex doesn't have to call Susan. She calls him the very same night as their Bear Mountain date. *Now what do I do?* he thinks. *She won't let up for a minute—what's her problem? Surely if sex is all she wanted, she could get picked up by any guy, anywhere, do it, and then move on. Could it be that she really loves me or that she is so strongly attracted to me that she must consummate our relationship? Yeah. Hello!* reality chimes in.

That week it snows very hard, and on Saturday, the GSP is essentially unplowed and closed having almost two feet of snow on it. Although Alex has made no plans to see Susan due to the inclement weather, once again he is drawn to her as if she had cast a voodoo spell upon him. He gets into his 4WD Nissan truck and enters the access road to the GSP. To no one's surprise, the parkway is completely empty except for him. The compact blue truck geared in 4WD high is cutting a path in the snowfield en route to Susan's apartment. He reaches her exit, pays the toll, and heads for his little miss dangerous. The excitement is overpowering the fear as he marches onward to her silent calling.

Arriving at her apartment, Alex bangs on the door. Susan spread the floral door curtains to see who it is. She is surprised to see Alex standing there and immediately lets him inside. She appears happy that he has come to see her in such bad weather. There is no sign of anyone else having been there; they are alone. She gives him a sweet kiss and big hug while he still has his coat on. Alex is sporting a pair of full-length embroidered leather cowboy boots. Susan approves by saying, "I like your fancy, western boots. They make you look even taller." She did advertise for a SWPM at 6'+. It must make her feel powerful to be able to have all her needs and wants satisfied by a big guy, Alex contemplates. It is amazing how a desirable woman can manipulate a man so easily. She is clearly emerging as the boss of this relationship, and now Alex is the obedient puppy dog.

Fearing that the foreplay already started will lead to his ultimate humiliation, ED, Alex quickly suggests that they go bowling at the alleys up the block, if they are open in this drastic weather. Coats and boots go on as the couple prepares themselves for the storm outside.

The bowling alley is open, but Sue and Alex are the only two people there besides the desk clerk. He rents two pairs of bowling shoes and secures alley #8. Susan had indicated in her voice mailbox greeting that she liked bowling, Alex recalls. He watches her approach on the alley, and her form is quite good. She throws a slow rolling ten-pounder but gets a strike. To share her momentary joy, she hurries back to Alex at the scorekeeper's desk and gives him a big hug around his neck. Alex can't help but think that she is what he has wanted all his life. She cuts a sweet image in her black spandex pants and pink Sassoon sweatshirt, looking like a native-born westerner.

After three games each, the couple gets ready to leave the alleys. As Alex and Sue are standing at the cashiers counter, the attendant looks at Alex then at Sue then back at Alex but says nothing. He has expressed his disappointment of this racially mixed couple without saying a word. Alex shrugs it off. As long as nothing was said to insult them, he can handle the looks and remain calm. This is quite unlike the encounter on Perkins's overlook; no need for self-defense here, no need at all.

The couple leaves the building, slosh their way through the heavy, wet snow, and get back into the truck. *Now what?* Alex thinks then says "Lunch?"

Sue quickly returns, "No, let's go back to my apartment and I'll make a Chinese lunch for you."

Johnson chimes in, *I bet I know what she has in mind for dessert.*

Shut up, Johnson, says Alex silently.

Back at her apartment, Sue warms up a variety of Chinese delicacies that she has brought home from the takeout restaurant at which she works. Every one is delicious. Alex has been doing Chinese food, Americanized of course, since he was fourteen. There was a Chinese restaurant one-half block from his high school grounds named Sal Gordon's—how very un-Chinese.

After finishing the equivalent of a dim sum meal, the two are thinking the same thing: it's time for some sexual activity. As Susan walks by Alex, he reaches for her, and she positions herself between his legs. He is sitting on a kitchen table chair, and she is standing. Their height differences align her covered breasts with his face. They start to kiss, and Alex has his hands on her petite but tight buttocks that are wrapped in black spandex. Her shirt is buttoned up to the neck exposing no sign of breasts. Alex is about to face his greatest fear. He is kissing her body in the area between her breasts and caressing her buttocks gently. Finally, thoughtlessly, he makes his move ever so subtly by directing his kisses from between her covered breasts to over her left breast. Within a microsecond, Susan responds with a sigh of pleasure and moves from between his legs holding his hand while motioning him to get up and go over to the bed with her. She walks him to the bed and lies down on it facing him. Susan unbuttons the top of her blouse as Alex lies alongside her, thinking, *Uh-oh, now I've really done it.* She begins her deadly formation of suction tongue kissing, and Alex unbuttons her shirt completely kissing her bra-covered breasts. In a flash, she disappears her bra, and Alex has the pleasure of seeing a perfectly proportional and matched set of her small exactly round breasts with substantial nipples. A draftsman couldn't have made more perfect spheres than these tantalizing petite vanilla fudge sundaes with a cherry on top of each. Alex instinctively indulges himself and begins to fondle and suck on them to her complete delight. He is enjoying this activity so much that Johnson starts to respond getting about halfway there instinctively. As Alex realizes what Johnson is doing, Johnson suddenly becomes detached from Alex's activities and becomes numb, deflating and starting to recede back into his shell. Alex feels nothing now as Johnson has gone into the fail-safe mode. He begins to get panicky and starts to sweat.

Sensing something, Susan asks, "What's the matter?"

"Nothing's the matter," replies Alex as he continues to caress her breasts but has no desire whatsoever to continue this activity. Susan pushes his hand down toward her genitals, and he responds by caressing them through the spandex. She realigns his hand under the spandex, but it's too tight a fit for his hand. Instantaneously, resourceful Susan relocates her spandex pants about a foot lower than her privates exposing her transparent panties. Alex robotically reaches down and puts his finger inside her imitating the sex act. She starts to moan a little bit, and in a few minutes, she reaches orgasm. Johnson, meanwhile, is asleep and in hiding.

Now she feels obligated, and she wants to pleasure Alex. She reaches for his pants and starts to unzip them when Alex says, "No, don't." Susan quickly grunts and frets like a little girl just deprived of her favorite candy. As she persists, Alex finally faces the moment of truth and allows her to unfasten his pants and pull them and his underwear down about a foot. There, in broad daylight, in all his glory, is Johnson—completely limp, fully numbed, and asleep. Alex, while turning different shades of red and sweating profusely, quickly replies, "I guess that I am not ready for you yet." This is damage control implying that more foreplay is needed to get Johnson to respond. Unphased by his limpness, Susan straddles him as he lies on his back and he sees her in her beautiful nakedness—a perfect little body other men would kill for, or be killed for. Her satiny black hair tops off her very desirable body.

After about ten minutes of this Chinese torture of desiring to enter her but being unable to, Alex gets up and apologizes, thus feeling like a useless piece of shit. Susan says to him, "You've made me very happy today," referring to the one orgasm which Alex caused this multi-orgasmic petite doll to have.

This session ends without further naked encounters, and Alex has sunk into a deep depression over his failure to perform. More "good times" are ahead for Susan as she just writes this off as "too soon" and "too little" stimulation to get him hard. She will ultimately realize that even she, with all her physical gifts, will be unable to unlock Johnson from the fail-safe mode. Alex will be referred to her "associates" again.

12

THE HOMECOMING OR MAYBE THIS TIME WILL BE A GO

Alex continues to beat himself up for about four days, but when Susan continues to call every night, he feels relieved. Maybe he'll get another chance after all. All concepts of what's morally right and wrong have grayed out at this point. Alex is preoccupied with how to satisfy Susan and overcoming his ED. He continues to send her flowers and treat her like a lady. Even though he didn't perform last weekend, she is still interested because she has fallen in love too with Alex's gentle and gentlemen-like ways (he hopes).

This weekend, Alex arranges to pick her up on Saturday and bring her to his house for the weekend. He is both nervous and excited, hoping for the best, i.e., normal sexual intercourse. It snows heavily that week clogging Alex's driveway and causing him to park his 4WD truck at the edge of his driveway, not even able to negotiate the long path to his garage with 4WD.

Saturday comes quickly, and the "big weekend" begins. When Alex and Sue reach his house, she puts on the required rubber boots to hoof it up the seventy-five-foot driveway to the garage entrance. Once the nickel tour of the house is complete, Alex puts on a Chicago CD and plays the romantic "If You Leave Me Now" track. They sit on the love seat in his parlor, and Alex says, "Susan, if we stay together or get married, I want your son, Tao, to live here with us. He'll be my son too." Alex must have hit a nerve in Susan as she begins to cry. He holds her tight, and the two are silent for the moment.

Susan is thinking, *How can I hurt this nice guy who evens loves my son before he has even met him?* But given the circumstances and conditions of her employment by Ping, the only way that Tao will not be hurt is if she infects Alex. She cannot fall in love with him and accomplish her goal. One way or the other, Alex is as good as dead already.

Since it is only early afternoon, Alex suggests that they go bowling then get lunch. He kisses her tears and dries her eyes, and they plow through the two feet of snow in the driveway back out to the truck. The alleys are about a twenty-minute ride; in fact, everything is about a twenty-minute ride from Alex's house that is buried deep in the woods. Again at the cashier's desk in the alleys after bowling, Alex hands the money to the attendant who looks at him, then at her, and then back at him without saying a word. More racial profiling which the couple just blows off. Next door to the bowling complex is an Italian restaurant where the couple has a pleasant more or less non-discriminatory lunch since the joint is almost empty on this foul weather day. After lunch, the couple goes back to Alex's house, and it, being winter, is already dark. They will be in the house for the rest of this Saturday.

"Time for a shower," Alex announces. "How about it, Susan, do you want to take a shower with me?"

She says, "I took one this morning, but I guess I'm taking another one now."

Both get naked and enter the shower. He washes her back then gently begins to do her female parts. Johnson is being aroused by this activity and the constant kissing in the shower as well as by her washing and pulling on him. To Alex's delight, he gets about three-fourths ready. They try to put him in, but he's still too cheese-like soft. Now he begins to deflate and get numb again. After the mutual toweling and caressing, the couple put on their bedclothes. These consist of underwear for him and a loose night sheet and skimpy panties for her. They get into his bed, and the caressing gets more serious. She is lying flat on her back with him alongside her. She sucks face and darts her tongue around his open mouth. Then Alex caresses her perfectly circular breasts and starts to suck on her erect oversized nipples while she clears the obstacle nightshirt out of his way. She is moaning a little bit by now. Sue again directs his hand down to her genitals, and Alex has no choice but to comply. Johnson has receded into slumber, so the hand and the fingers will have the task of attempting to satisfy her. He probes inside her and finds a wet and warm environment. She quickly comes to climax with a shudder as he stimulates her clit. A few microseconds after completion, to Alex's surprise, she continues unabatedly kissing him and now starts to suck on his tongue. Still, Johnson is locked in the fail-safe mode. For the second time in as many minutes, she places his hand in her, and Alex repeats the in and out mimicking along with doing flickers. She moans again as he moves his middle finger up and down like he would do with Johnson if the pain in the ass ever woke up. The moaning gets very loud, and she climaxes again. Now Alex feels that this would surely have satisfied her and she'll cool down. Wrong! Round three—bong! She is still kissing him then guides his mouth to her right breast, nipple still erect and hard as granite. Down to her wetness below once again his hand is guided. Like a trained seal, he enters her with two fingers and manipulates her tiny pleasure center. More moaning then she releases again once more achieving orgasm. Three times in about fifteen minutes! Isn't that a Guinness world record or something? Alex has no bank of data for this type of woman; no wonder there are so many Chinese people.

Smiling with the devilish look of just having been pleasured, Susan reaches down to gently grab hold of Johnson who is hiding behind some pubic hair. She takes some baby oil into her other hand then rubs both hands together. She begins stroking Johnson, and he becomes somewhat excited but not firm. The frequency of her stroking increases in magnitude, and the tightness of her hold strengthens. Alex starts to tense his buttocks muscles to enhance the chance of coming. Feeling the bed shake, she says, "What are you doing?"

He replies, "Trying to help you make me reach orgasm." She continues and succeeds in her work as Alex, still not really hard, comes in her hand. Smiling, she shows her wet hand to Alex and says, "Which one will be our daughter?" referring to the semen on her hand. Alex is too exhausted to reply to her joking. He lies there completely naked with her but totally detached and disappointed that he has again failed. His depression is growing by leaps and bounds. Unbeknownst to him at this time is the fact that his softness just saved his life, again.

Early the next morning, Alex wakes up, and he is hard as hard can be. He takes Susan's hand and places it on Johnson. She smiles with approval and eagerness. Then, by now Alex being fully conscious, feels Johnson melt back into his pubic hair. Johnson has cheesed out on him again. What tremendous frustration!

Susan asks him, "Why didn't you put him inside me when he was so hard?"

Gentleman Alex sincerely replies, "Because you were not ready for him. You were not stimulated yet to wetness." It would be like rape. He couldn't even think of hurting her even if it meant being successfully inside her. Susan sits silently frustrated as well since she just can't seem to infect this guy and is feeling more and more less compassionate for him and his "problem." What to do? How can she not hurt him and simultaneously reach her quota? She has been with just him for over a month, and she is falling dangerously behind. Dangerous for her, dangerous for her son, and dangerous for her imprisoned parents.

Susan and Alex get out of his fifty-year-old truly antique bed without any further sexual activity on this cold, cloudy morning in March. She has to go to work at the restaurant today at noon, so she starts to pretty herself up. Alex towers over her in the bathroom mirror so much that he is sprucing up using the same cabinet mirror. He is not a morning person, never was, ergo he's ready to go in less than ten minutes. Sex is the furthest thing from his mind in the early a.m. hours. Susan, on the other hand, is constantly horny and ready. Alex again regrets that he is not nineteen again when he could do it three or four times in a couple of hours. Wrong time, right place. At nineteen, it was right time, wrong place.

As Alex combs his hair (in back of Susan at the mirror), he notices how pretty she really is, especially her radically slanted brown-black eyes. She is dressed to kill (literally) with a petite size 3 mini-skirt and white blouse as always, laced and buttoned up to the top. How well he knows now what a dynamite little package of perfect breasts are well concealed under her blouse. After a bit more makeup, she is ready to go. She takes some ice cream and a Hershey bar (with nuts) for her breakfast en route to work. Alex picks her up at her petite apartment and drives her to his house; now he will drop her off directly at work some sixty miles down the road. He'll kill some time around Bergen, Essex, and Passaic counties then return to pick her up at 8:00 p.m. at her Chinese takeout joint and drive her home.

As he drops her off at work, she kisses him very lightly on the lips quickly so as not to be "caught" by someone. There are only lips sans the suction and the perky tongue. Susan is being extremely discrete about this affair and will show no public display of affection (PDAs) except for holding hands in remote places. It won't be long now till Alex will receive no affection public or private from her. She has made her decision to dump him before she falls in love with this tall handsome Polish American who has treated her like a princess.

13

THE FINAL WEEKEND—GOODBYE, ALEX

The nightly phone calls continue unabated this week, but Alex has noticed that her phone is busy quite often as he tries to call. For that matter, she received an awful lot of calls every time he stayed at her apartment until she switched the phone off. Popular girl for a foreigner not going to school. He didn't realize it at the time, but most of those calls were from other men pursuing her. One was her ex-Chinese-boyfriend whom she despised because he treated her like the little whore that she was. She even told Alex about him and used him as the reason why she was advertising for an American man. Susan also mentioned that she had had a black boyfriend. When Alex asked her, "Was it a sexual relationship?" She answered yes without any hesitation or guilt in her voice. Once, she said, "We did it seven times in a few hours, four times before the movies, and three times after when we got back here." When Alex asked her why she broke it off, she said because she couldn't marry him or even be seen with him in China. She would be disgraced in her homeland for associating with a black man.

This greatly upset Alex who was now getting glimpses of this woman as she really was and not as a candidate for a wife and mother of his children. Although he was never taught to be racist by his parents since they grew up in a poor neighborhood in Passaic with blacks, this black boyfriend whom she had "good sex" with (her words) really bothered Alex. The image of some middle-aged black guy having "good sex" with his China doll when he couldn't even have quick sex one time in one day was very upsetting.

Little Ms. Snow White was really little Miss Dangerous. She never even suggested to Alex that he should use a condom, not even at the beginning when she didn't know about his "problem." Just how many guys had been intimate with this gal anyway? Stranger than that, he swore to accept the black relationship by virtue of being a Christian and still was very much in love with her. Anytime he brought the matter about other guys up, she would get nearly violent and say that there's nothing wrong with having good sex without any strings; she had good sex with her ex-Chinese-boyfriend too! She certainly did not have good sex with Alex; theoretically, he did not have sex with her at all (just like Billy C.). After all these elongated discussions, what could he expect this weekend?

It came around very fast, that is, the next weekend. Alex was in a quandary as he drove over to her apartment not knowing what to exactly expect, but hoping she was still interested in him. He gave off a sigh of relief when others would curse when he found out that it was her time of the month; the pressure to perform would be absent. But then again, with her insatiable appetite for sex, maybe things will get messy, bloody. No way will he get involved in that scene. As long as it was her blood and it stayed with her, Alex would be all right.

As usual, Alex goes up the back staircase that badly needs to be painted and approaches her six light door. He looks through the open curtains and sees Susan talking on her no-frills black phone.

She seems to be arguing with someone. Since Alex doesn't understand Mandarin, all he can discern is that she is very upset, crying and yelling into the receiver at the same time. He thinks, *Maybe I should go. This doesn't look like a good time to see her. But I can't leave. I promised to be here at noon, and her kitchen clock already reads twelve fifteen.* With an end to contemplation and a decision made, Alex steps back away from the window and knocks on her door. Susan is startled by the tapping and quickly dries her eyes then hangs up the phone. She comes to the brown entrance door and peeks through her yellow flowered curtains then smiles at Alex. The door is quickly opened, and she lurches at him to give him a big hug and kiss but falls flat on her face. Alex was taken off guard by her "attack" expecting to see some kind of pointed weapon. He apologizes as he helps her to her feet claiming that he slipped on the little bit of snow on the back porch. She is wearing a bathrobe with just underwear underneath. Alex thinks, *I hope this doesn't get messy.* He is immediately relieved as she walks inside with him, locks the door, draws the curtains, and sheds her bathrobe. There in the center of her dimly lit kitchen, she is standing topless with just a pair of transparent pink silk panties under which is an absorbent pad.

Susan announces, "I have my period today, so I'm not feeling well. Why don't we just stay here and watch your videos (the VCR tapes that he lent her)?"

"Okay. Sounds good to me. Aren't you cold with just underwear on?" he inquires.

"No. I'm warm. I like to dress like this when I'm home. It makes me feel free! Give me your jacket and lie down on the bed while I get the videos," she remarks.

Alex asks, "Which one do you want to watch?"

She answers, "*Dances with Wolves*. I watched it but didn't understand. You can explain it to me while we watch it together." Her perfect little rotund breasts don't even shake when she bounces onto the bed. No excess flab here, just two prime-size grade A lollipops; one flesh colored with a cherry on top, the other an unbelievable mirror image. God created a perfectly matched set; these are the nicest breasts on the planet. Frank Purdue, eat your heart out! But will she let me play with them if the warm-up leads to a closed playground? Susan's playground—closed for repairs, monthly.

Susan lies alongside Alex but does nothing to encourage him as if two naked breasts constitute nothing. As the movies plays, out of the blue she says, "I've decided that I am going to cure your problem," referring to his ED.

Alex is pleasantly stunned! He thinks to himself, *I must have died and went to heaven. This beautiful little doll is going to work with me to help me have normal sexual relations with her. Then we'll get married and have a family. Everything is working out great, couldn't be better. Unbelievable!*

During *Dances with Wolves*, Susan continually is asking, "Why? Why did they kill the wolf? Why are they hurting him? Why this, why that?" Finally she backs off from her asking why then says, "I have to go to sleep now because I'm working tomorrow."

Alex, trying to be understanding, says, "Okay. It's late. Let's go to sleep."

She turns off the thirteen-inch color TV and lights and lies on the left side of her queen mattress with her back facing Alex. He senses a sudden coolness, aloofness. Something has turned her one hundred eighty degrees around to completely cold to him. He asks, "Something wrong?"

She says, "No."

Alex then asks, "Do you mind if I put my arm around you and hold you while you sleep?"

Coolly she says, "It doesn't matter to me. You can put your arm around me if you want."

He feels a little relieved. Maybe she's just tired and out of sorts because of her period. Alex will not forget this night as his racing mind allows him to half sleep maybe an hour or so.

The next morning the alarm wakes her up, and she curses at the clock. "Stupid clock!" she says.

As she gets dressed in a pair of very tight black jeans, Alex is sensing an attitude, an air of indifference toward him. He sees it in her body language more than hearing it in her words. Alex says, "I'll call you tonight after work around nine, okay?"

Rather indifferently, she answers, "Okay." They leave the apartment together with no goodbye kiss, hug, or anything of affection that might predict a future in their relationship. Susan gets in her Nissan and drives to work; Alex gets in his truck and goes home.

Nine o'clock has arrived slowly but surely for Alex. He suspects that something is wrong; something is missing like when you leave your house feeling that you forgot to do something, like turn off the gas or shut the water faucet. Alex calls Susan, but there's no answer. The angst builds inside of him. He calls again fifteen minutes later, and the line is busy—good, she's home. A half hour later, the line is still busy. Alex finally gets through around 10:00 p.m., and Susan is speaking very composed, softly, and demurely. After the usual "How was your day" small talk is done, she says out of the blue, "I don't want go out with you anymore."

Alex is floored. He quickly replies, "Why? What did I do?"

She says that she cannot explain it in English. She is going to put her ad back in the *Star-Ledger*. Alex is crying while he tries to change her mind, but then she starts crying too and replies, "I don't want hurt you."

He says, "You're hurting me now by leaving when I don't know why." His pleading fails to change her mind, and she says goodbye to him. Alex, still crying, hangs up the phone saying to himself, *I knew something wasn't right with her sudden change in disposition last night. It has to be my ED, but she said she was going to cure me. What or who changed her mind?* Wiping his eyes, Alex is miserable as if one of his animals had died. He loved his cats of which he had two; fortunately they were both young, two to three years old each. He loved all animals because he spent nine years in virtual isolation due to his undiagnosed panic disorder when his friends abandoned him, and only his animals stayed and never stopped loving him.

What am I going to do? We were supposed to go to Virginia next weekend for my niece's baby shower. I loved her, and she callously dumped me. I'm miserable.

Alex took a sick day on Monday still very upset about losing his little China doll. To add more misery to his present unhappy state, he found her ad back in the paper on the following Thursday. Now he knew it was over. His attitude begins to switch to a survivor mode. *That little slut didn't waste any time looking for a new boyfriend. Long-term relation leading to marriage, my ass. She just wants to get laid and as often as possible. Sex is her drug. It controls her. She's not the right girl for me. Do I want a whore for a wife? Even an ex-whore would have a tough time changing roles to mother and wife. God has actually saved me from a bad association, but it still hurts when I think of her. She was such a doll!*

Something's going on here that doesn't meet the eye or ear, and I will get to the bottom of this. With that, Alex goes to Virginia alone the next weekend to be with his niece and her husband on their happy occasion. This isn't the end of the road for him. He has too much self-respect. He did nothing wrong.

14

ALEX GOES TO VIRGINIA, ALONE

Dr. Supenski has a dual mission in Virginia: go to the USPTO in Arlington to defend a patent application which he wrote and attend his niece's baby shower on the outskirts of Front Royal, Virginia. The original plan was to take Susan with him and share the driving of her car since she couldn't drive his stick shift vehicles. They were to check into the Super Starlight Motel in Front Royal late Thursday so that Alex could get up about 8:30 a.m. the next morning, shave, shower, and be at the USPTO by 10:30 a.m., some sixty-five miles away. There in the maze of concrete buildings he would park his car in a municipal garage below the USPTO, ride the elevator to the third floor, and link up at room 306 with his supervisor, Dr. George Pilatus, who was flying into Dulles airport that morning.

Five hours on the interstate highway system gives a man a lot of time to reflect. Alex developed a scathing mental text to send to Susan once he reached the motel and checked in, that is, in between tears of sadness. Ruminating about how he would construct the letter and what possible affect it would have, he is interrupted in Maryland by construction that slows him to a crawl. He can smell the strong odor of manured cornfields this April day as the local farmers begins to prepare their soils for planting. He flashes back to a simpler time in his life when he was a boy helping out his Uncle Stanley on his one-hundred-twenty-acre farm of rolling hills in Orangeburg, NY. On those hot, humid summer days, he used to herd the black and white Jersey cows into the well-weathered gray barn and guide them into their stalls. In front of each cow were raised water and food dishes; the cow could activate and fill the water dish by pushing her jaw down on it. They were milked twice a day, once at 5:00 a.m. and again at 5:00 p.m. Behind the cows was a twelve-inch trough running the length of the barn where the stalls were called the manure pit. One of Alex's jobs was to use a spade to move the inaccurately plopped manure that missed the pit into it. Then, after the cows were milked and sent out to pasture, he had to shovel the manure out of the pit and into a large hanging bucket suspended on a track that ran the filled bucket outside the barn. There, strategically located in the barnyard, was the manure spreader where he dumped the bucket loads. This was an early introduction to a recycling process for Alex.

When following (guiding) the cows out to pasture, he would be gifted with cow pies as the animals relieved themselves as needed. He and his cousins of about the same age would walk barefoot and step right into the warm manure. Although revolting to Alex now, it didn't seem so then. Conceptions of events change with time even when the events are superficially identical.

Alex suddenly returns to the highway mentally and realizes that he feels much better after his mental excursion into the treasured past. He takes the exit for Winchester and arrives at the Starlight Motel around 8:00 p.m. After checking in, he goes to his second-story room, 256, and keys the door. It's his practice not to take a ground-floor room because anybody could jigger the double glass door lock and enter in the middle of the night. Also, everybody and anybody can see you walking around in your underwear if you forget to draw the drapes. After some nightly routines, he hops in bed and puts on the boob tube, sets the timer for two hours, and gradually falls asleep in that time.

Friday morning the telephone rings at 6:40 a.m. Alex picks up the receiver and blurts out groggily, "Yeah."

"It's eight thirty. You should be on your way to Arlington, Mr. Supenski," states the desk clerk.

Alex looks at the clock radio and sees that the clerk has read the hands on his clock reversed. He says, "Thank you, but its only 6:40 a.m."

"So sorry, sir, I must have misread my watch. Sorry!" chimes the clerk.

Alex just about falls back asleep when he hears someone jiggling a key in his door. He thinks, *This is not good unless maid service is very early in this motel.* He gets out of bed, puts on his pants, and stations himself so that he is behind the door when it opens. Very quietly, Tao with two associates, Ming and Zhang, begins to enter the room. As Tao is just past the door entrance, Alex kick-slams the door in the faces of Ming and Zhang then quickly deadbolts the door as Tao is picking himself up off the floor. Alex is as enraged as a Bengal tiger whose zebra lunch just escaped his pursuit. Tao pulls out his Sig with silencer, but within less than a second, Alex wheel-kicks the gun out of his hand, and it bounces under the walnut dresser out of Tao's reach. Tao lurches forward toward Alex with a punch-kick combination only to find that Alex is not there as the beige wall gets kicked and punched. As Tao turns around, Alex clocks him with a much-focused lunge punch knuckle sandwich right in the mouth knocking out several of Tao's former permanent teeth. He then grabs the stunned Chinaman and smashes his head into the television. As Tao gets back to his feet dazed, he feels a powerful spinning back kick catch him in the solar plexus sending him crashing through the window, down two stories, and into the pool. His two associates outside the door hear police sirens and quickly disappear. They retrieve

Tao from the bloodied pool and speed out of the parking lot, tires squealing down Route 156. About five minutes later, the Virginia state police arrive.

Alex is sitting on the bed with his heart and mind racing. *What the hell is going on here?* he asks himself. *I don't know anyone of the Asian persuasion that would want me dead, do I? Maybe that was Susan's ex-husband, but isn't this behavior a little extreme?*

Just then, the police bang on the bolted door and shout, "State police, open up!" Alex opens the door to see two cops pointing drawn guns at him. "Get down on the floor, do it, NOW!" one of the cops shouts. Alex complies and lies down on the bloody carpet while one cop handcuffs him then stands him up. The other cop sees the Sig 9 mm that Tao "dropped" and picks it up with a pencil through the trigger loop and bags it.

As the cops escort Alex out to the patrol car, the hotel manager informs them that he is a guest there. Noting this, the state police take him to the Front Royal police headquarters. The tan colonial brick building with two Roman pillars in front has just opened for business at the present time of 7:00 a.m. Alex is brought through a side door, fingerprinted, then taken directly to the interrogation room. The drab green ten-by-ten-foot room has a one-way see-through glass on one wall. Detective La Plaka begins the questioning. "Is this your 9 mm handgun?"

Alex answers, "No. I wouldn't buy a Sig. They tend to jam too much."

An aide walks into the room and whispers something to La Plaka. La Plaka starts to realize that maybe he is interrogating the victim rather than the perpetrator of the crime.

"What happened back there in the motel?" La Plaka asks.

Alex replies, "Some Asian guy whom I've never met tried to kill me. If the desk clerk hadn't misread his watch and didn't call me at 6:40 a.m., I would have been sound asleep, and the perp might have succeeded. I'll tell you that I'm not impressed with the level of safety in this part of Virginia and probably won't plan on vacationing here in the future. Also, I would appreciate it if you could get me out of here quickly since I've got sixty miles to drive to get to Arlington to defend a patent application. If I'm late or don't show, I may lose my job."

La Plaka leaves the room to consult with forensics and ballistics. Joe Michaels, forensic scientist, tells him that no prints on the gun match Alex's. A ballistics report faxed in from Staten Island upon Joe's request shows the same print is a Glock 19 that was used in a murder there last week of a highly respected Caucasian English professor. La Plaka noted the extensive academic background of Alex in an earlier report and concludes that they have an oriental serial killer on their hands. Targeting PhDs, or so it seems. La Plaka goes back into the green room. He stares at Alex momentarily then says, "Your credentials and statements check out, but we need you to fill in some forms for the crime report, look at some mug shots, and answer a few more questions. We'll helicopter you to Arlington so you'll be on time for your meeting."

Alex is impressed but then asks, "How do I get back here after the patent examiner is through with me?" La Plaka tells Alex that the copter will wait at the USPTO helipad till he's done then fly him back to Front Royal to look at some more mugs shots of possible perps.

Alex isn't crazy about flying in helicopters, but that's the only way he can make it on time to the USPTO. La Plaka takes him back to the motel so he can get his paperwork and briefcase and change into some presentable clothes. The state police helicopter lands in the motel lot that is pretty much vacant at this point. Alex is feeling real queasy and nauseous as the bubbled bird lifts off the ground and negotiates a hard left turn. He starts to dry heave and grabs the copter barf bag. Nothing went in this morning, so nothing comes out. The pilot gives him some Dramamine and a Xanax tablet with a bottle of Poland Spring. Alex takes the Xanax and starts to doze a little.

In less than thirty minutes, the pilot lands the helicopter on the helipad on the roof of the USPTO. Right on time! Alex wakes up with a start, yawns, and gets his things together. He deplanes and enters the roof exit door, walks up to the elevator, and presses floor 3. The sudden sensation of the elevator dropping quickly to reach the third floor brings back the nausea. The elevator stops, and Alex composes himself and exits to the hallway in search of room 306. When he arrives there, he raps on the glass in the door meekly and hears a booming "Enter!"

The patent examiner has a stern look like the 6'4", 275 lb. priest disciplinarian Alex barely survived in high school. One thing Father taught him was discipline and how to take a punch, kick, slap, and hair or ear lobe pull in the name of discipline.

Dr. Pilatus is already in the room as is a patent agent whom Monochrome (Alex's firm) hired to rework the text to a more acceptable format for the patent office. The Monochrome lawyers were a real bunch of overpaid losers who didn't know shit from Shinola when it came to scientific writing, and Alex had to write the first two drafts himself.

Despite the presence of the agent and Pilatus, the brunt of defending this patent application fell upon Alex who had to refute why the seven patents cited against his work as essentially the same invention as his patent application were, in fact, not the same. He had to demonstrate the novelty and usefulness of his work to the patent examiner.

Two and one half hours later with several more process claims added by the patent agent, the examiner accepted the application as novel and useful provided that Alex rewrite the "old art" parts emphasizing his new art. The patent which would result would be very narrow in scope but would allow Monochrome to make a high contrast color film similar to those films of the big guys viz: Kodak and Fuji. Mission accomplished!

Alex rejected Pilatus's offer for lunch claiming that he had to get back to Front Royal to settle some police business. Pilatus exclaimed, "WHAT!" out of complete shock. Alex ensures him that it's no big deal and he'll explain fully when he gets back to work next Monday.

On the helicopter trip back, the nausea is replaced with a fear and tremendous anxiety caused by the attempt on his life. Alex decides that he will contact Sensei Thomas and his dojo friends and try to enlist their help. This karate brotherhood is stronger than genetic brotherhood because the brothers all faced combat together not unlike military combat in a war zone.

Sensei Thomas has moved to Florida, so Alex will need to call his original NJ dojo to get his address and phone number. The Van deGraff brothers and several cop friends will also be summoned. If these Chinese guys want to start trouble, the brotherhood (kyokai) will settle it, permanently.

Alex is dropped off at the motel lot by the copter and gets into a waiting patrol car. The FBI has become involved since an interstate crime has been attempted and committed in the case of CJ of SI with a possible link to a suspected national conspiracy.

Alex sits down in the Front Royal patrol car and shakes hands with Agent Barilla, a stocky tan-skinned well-built young man of Italian heritage. He sports jet-black hair and a neatly trimmed matching black mustache. While talking en route to police headquarters, Alex learns that Agent Barilla is also a black belt in aikido and a marksman-level shooter, top of his graduating class at the academy after Harvard Law School. The two men take an instant liking to one another being kindred spirits of sorts. Barilla says confidently, "Don't worry, Alex, we'll get this guy and put a mean hurt on him and any of his associates involved in this before they are extradited. The Chinese government may get them back one piece at a time."

Alex laughs out loud then thinks, *It feels good to laugh again after all the shit that went down today. I feel much better already.*

15

TAO BACK IN CHINATOWN FROM VIRGINIA

Ming and Zhang leave Virginia that same day as the attack on Alex. While Ming drives, Zhang tries to nurse his boss, Tao, who is in fairly bad shape after Alex's beating. His jaw is broken, four teeth are gone, and he has severe lacerations on his skull and suffered a broken collarbone as a result of the two-story fall at the Starlight Motel. Blood is all over the back seat and floor staining the beige carpeting a deep pink. Zhang gives Tao some opium to ease his pain on the six-hour return trip to NYC.

As they stop at the tollbooth on the Goethals Bridge, the attendant takes their four dollars without comment, not even a "Thank you" or "Have a nice day." As the gray Nissan approaches the bridge, the toll collector alerts the NJ state police that a gray Sentra with NJ license plate ZSF-681 has an injured person with extensive bleeding in the rear seat. The occupants are three male Orientals and seem very suspicious.

By the time the NJ state cops can respond, Tao and associates are already on the Verrazano out of an NJ cop's jurisdiction. They radio the NYPD in both Brooklyn and lower Manhattan, suspecting that the three male Orientals may be heading for Chinatown to blend in and vanish; this is a common ploy for illegal Chinese in the USA. As the Chinamen cross the Brooklyn Bridge into lower Manhattan, they see that four NYPD police cars with at least as many cops have set up a checkpoint going into Manhattan. Ming panics and floors the accelerator to crash through the police barricade. Two NYPD blue and whites start the pursuit as Ming races down FDR Drive weaving in and out of traffic in an attempt to lose the cops. He exits to 34th Street and shoots across town toward Broadway. The cops follow suit but get momentarily blocked by a sanitation truck backing up causing them to lose Ming. The adrenalin is coursing in Ming's body as he makes two sequential sets of left then right turns at high speed nearly smashing into a dozen sidewalk citizens of Metropolis. Suddenly, Ming slows down to the speed limit and behaves like a good citizen with a front-end damaged gray car. In New York, this damaged vehicle is one of hundreds, so no one pays particular notice to it. Traveling down 7th Ave into SoHo, Ming negotiates the car onto York Street and into the dimly lit alleyway next to Tao's apartment killing the lights as he enters. Zhang shoulders Tao to his apartment while Ming covers the car with a black tarp. The gray Nissan nearly disappears from a Canal Street view with the black tarp in the now dark alleyway. Ming rushes upstairs to help Zhang with Tao. He enters the small but functional apartment and calls Dr. Chan who rushes to their location to treat Tao.

After Chan examines Tao, he silently concludes that Tao can be of no further use to the program and needs to be expunged since his fame has made him a wanted, well-described fugitive. However, no one is allowed, not even a top operative, to pull the plug on another operative without specific permission from the chairman. Claiming that he needs to consult an online medical text to treat Tao properly, Dr. Chan boots up Tao's Microwest computer. Typing in a bypass emergency code, he is now in direct contact with Ping without Zhang, Ming, or Tao aware of it. Using an obscure medical code known only by Ping's top operatives and for which Ping has a translating device on his computer, Chan describes Tao's condition to Ping. Ping, in his best imitation of Al Capone, says on line, "Rub him out." The good doctor tells Zhang and Ming that Tao has lost a lot of blood and he is in critical condition requiring hospitalization. However, that is out of the question because hospitals must file reports of serious injuries with the police department. He dismisses Zhang and Ming telling them that he will do what he can for Tao and try to save his life. As the two Chinamen leave the apartment, Dr. Chan readies a syringe with potassium cyanide for Tao's "recovery." Within minutes, Tao is completely at rest as the lethal poison hits its mark. Chan leaves Tao's apartment after erasing any trace of him having been there by wiping the door handles, telephone with alcohol, and carrying the computer. As he passes Zhang and Ming on the street, he nods his head in the "No" direction and tells them to leave the area. He walks about four blocks uptown then hails a cab to take him near to his secret tunnel entrance to get back to his room under the beauty parlor. A few minutes later Dr. Chan exits the cab then leaves the computer in a sewer drain and gets on an uptown bus. About two city blocks from the beauty salon, he exits the bus and enters a phone booth. He calls the NYPD and gives them an anonymous tip that their Oriental fugitive was seen entering a building near Canal Street giving them the exact address. Strictly following Ping's orders, which Ping thought were brilliant, let NYC pay the funeral expenses; there's no way Ping can be associated with Tao's existence. The conspiracy was too tightly conceived and planned. The conspiracy continues unabated by the loss of one insignificant operative.

One thing continues to worry Ping, however, and that is how much Alex knows about his devious plot and whether he can recognize Zhang and Ming. If he can't eliminate the resilient Alex, he may have to retire Zhang and Ming; that would be tantamount to a defeat. Ping decides that he must get rid of Alex and fast; this American pig is a dangerous loose cannon.

16

ALEX BACK AT THE GOSHEN DOJO TO ENLIST HELP

After putting his white karate gi along with his black obi into a yellow-and-red Tommy Hilfiger gym bag, Alex straps the bag to the chrome luggage rack on his purple-and-white VT-1100 Honda Shadow. He backs the bike out of the garage working those dormant thigh muscles, closes the electronically controlled door, then hits the start button on the bike. The big V-twin roars to life emitting distinctly macho but toned-down exhaust notes. He was never into the super macho but deafening sounds of a Harley, although it did sound distinctively boss. After a full choke five-minute warm-up, Alex kicks up the stand then kicks down the gear lever into first using the brown Western boots that Susan thought so highly of; shit-stomping leather of the finest quality. A roll of the throttle and slow release of the clutch handle starts the pulsing machine down his driveway onto the brown dirt and rock road in front of the house. After five miles of sunny, verdant backcountry roads, which look like one continuous ping-pong tabletop, Alex reaches Interstate 78. It's a mostly tractor-trailer, light traffic early Saturday morning going east on 78. Kicking down through third into second gear and cranking the chrome-tipped throttle lever hard, Alex runs through second then third and into fourth gear in about five seconds accelerating the big twin pulsing heartbeat of the machine to 75 mph, the local flow rate this a.m. on Highway 78. He turns slightly left up the ramp over 78 to merge with the 287 north traffic. A yuppie in his latest toy, a Z3 BMW, damn near sideswipes him at the junction point of the ramp with 287. Alex shoulders the bike temporarily to let the second childhood jerk pass then reenters the right-most lane. Like the well-bred karateka he is, his driving is strictly defensive, so they'll be no chasing of the Beemer for reprisals.

Twenty minutes up 287 the highway junction with Interstate Route 80. Alex leans the bike into a right turn exit and enters the two-lane feeder. The traffic is heavy but moving at a brisk clip of 70 mph despite the posted double nickel speed limit. A state police black-and-white cruiser dusts him at an estimated speed around ninety without its lights and noisemakers on. The cop doesn't seem particularly interested in all the vehicles doing triple nickels plus ten.

The ride on Interstate Route 80 is through a particularly homely section of this cross-country highway. The twenty-foot-high concrete walls used to filter out noise from humanity also filter out any sign of non-vehicular life-forms as well. The need for the walls (at about million dollars per mile) serves as a continual source of debate between the taxpayers and the governor's office. Each new governor approves more walls as more of a jobs program than as a sound reduction project. Fortunately Mother Nature is hiding them slowly but surely by growing green multidirectional vines over them.

The final leg of the trip is through downtown Paterson which once served as a large industrial base within twenty miles of NYC. Now it serves as a particularly offensive onslaught to the senses attacking with sights and smells as rancid as a tube of spoiled goat cheese. Unfortunately, it must be traversed to get to the other side of the Passaic River, which in this area is Hawthorne where the Goshen Dojo is located. This ride, nearly complete, has taken Alex from the future into the past in a sense. Time consumed is roughly one hour from Alex's scenic isolated log cabin in Hunterdon County to the less scenic and overcrowded counties of Bergen and Passaic, the bedrooms for the New York City employees.

With the dojo just up ahead on the right, Alex downshifts the pulsing twin, brakes, and smoothly stops right at the front door where the bike will anxiously await the return of its owner for about two hours. It's a warm day, so the front door to the training center is wide open. Alex grabs his red-and-yellow gym bag and walks to the entrance. As soon as he enters, he stops, right foot to left and bows (rei) to the attendant black belt at the front desk, saying, "*Osu*, Yudansha Dennis."

Dennis returns the bow and is very surprised to see Nidan Alex. "Where the hell have you been all these years? We thought that you got deep-sixed in some war zone."

Alex responds, "The rumors of my death are greatly exaggerated. But I have had some real close calls lately, so I thought I'd better start working out with my kyokai brothers again. Some Chinese group is trying to kill me."

Dennis squints. "No bullshit, for real?"

"Unfortunately, yes, for real. Goshen-do has already saved my life twice. I think there is some sort of conspiracy against American professors going on, and it may involve some real pretty China dolls as a kind of bait. I'll be meeting another oriental gal in Staten Island shortly, you know, at Harrison College where that English professor was shot six times. She may have zero to do with this whole thing, but I am being especially cautious, and I need help from the brothers to watch my back. These guys are into 9 mm handguns and big knives, and last time I checked, I still needed more work on the speed bag to be faster than a speeding bullet," relates Alex.

Dennis throws out his open palm, and the two old friends squeeze palms securely. Then Dennis says, "You picked a good time to come back. Sensei Thomas is back in Jersey. Before he left for Florida, he did some detective work, and like with everything else Sensei does, he picked up excellent abilities in conventional weapons to add to his forte of Okinawan weapons. Your favorite was the bo, wasn't it?"

"You remember that shit after all these years? That's amazing, Dennis."

"I remember something else too. I remember that you were a damn good student and well-disciplined karateka. Everybody here felt a deep sense of loss when you stopped coming around to train. You know, for a big guy, you're all right," Dennis adds jokingly since he is only 5'4" and 110 lbs. himself. But don't be fooled by his size; he is one of the best fighters in the dojo working out seven days a week for at least five hours a day plus running the classes when Sensei is otherwise preoccupied.

At that point, Yudansha Ron Greater reis off the matted practice area into the foyer.

"Holy shit! Is that Alex Supenski in front of me, or is the light just getting to my eyes from him appearing and disappearing twenty years ago? Welcome back, buddy, where did you disappear to?" says Greater.

Dennis says, "Alex is in some deep shit with a Chinese gang. They tried to take him out twice already." Ron, being a cop in Bergen County, is quite used to trouble in his jurisdiction by gangs from Chinatown. He's already capped a couple and kicked several other asses while serving on the narcotics squad. One thing that all the kyokai members don't do is drugs; most of them don't drink anything stronger than 7UP. The chemicals interfere with the training program, and, as we all agree here, that's the only thing that matters to them, i.e., training and practicing karate. It's not just a martial art; it's a lifestyle.

Ron looks toward Alex and says, "You need help?" Alex is heartfelt amazed by this instant offer from a friend he hasn't seen in twenty years.

Then Dennis chimes, "I'm in."

A man couldn't ask for better brothers than this. These guys are willing to risk their lives to watch my back and help me save my own life, Alex thinks to himself.

Ron adds, "We'll get Cliff, Jerry, Doc, Frank, and some of the other yudanshas, and I guarantee we will put an end to this shit, Alex. From now on, one of us is going to be your backup twenty-four hours a day. Hell, sleeping is greatly overrated anyway, right, Dennis?"

"You're right," Dennis says. "I need to kick some real ass anyway. The practice dummies in the dojo don't fight back. This is going to be fun."

There, under the auspices of the pictures of the great Okinawan originators of what became Goshen-Do, the three men seal what amounts to a blood pact. An attack on one of the brothers is the same as an attack on all, and all will respond with a vengeance.

17

ALEX GOES TO MEET SI CHINA DOLL: LING

Alex was suspicious of Ling, and rightly so since professor CJ of SI claimed that he had been infected by her and that she never loved him. However, there was very little proof that Ling had anything to do with CJ's demise.

Ling had answered Alex's personal ad that he put into the *Star-Ledger* after the collapse of his relationship with Susan.

> SWPM, 6'3", 220#, blue eyes, brown hair, well-educated seeks Asian or Oriental SF for LTR leading to marriage and children.

Alex, in his taped greeting, mentioned that he was a PhD chemist who liked to read and ride his motorcycle because both helped him to escape the problems of everyday life and gave him a sense of freedom. He preferred petite, well-educated, pretty Asian women who were Christian.

Ling left her phone number in the voice mailbox assigned to Alex. She stated that she had most of what he sought and was "very pretty" and a PhD student in library science just completing her degree requirements at Columbia.

"Columbia!" Alex spoke out loud to himself. This girl must be really smart as well as beautiful. He arranges to meet her on the Harrison College campus for lunch during the week. At the time, Alex worked in Clark, NJ, so it was a relatively short trip past the garbage mounds just beyond the Outerbridge Crossing into Staten Island to get to Harrison College where Ling worked as an associate librarian. He was to meet her at the main library, and they would go to lunch somewhere.

Because of the possibility that Ling may be like Susan, i.e., addicted to sex with a possible in-country jealous ex-husband, Yudansha Ron Greater would meet him at the gate and follow him until he was safely back home.

Alex leaves Monochrome at 11:30 a.m. arriving at Harrison College at about 12:15 p.m. for his 12:30 p.m. lunch meeting with Ling. As he passes the entrance gate, he tells the guard that he's here to have lunch with the associate librarian, Ling. The silvered-hair old man waves him through directing him to the visitor's lot. Alex parks his car, a cobalt blue '92 Honda Accord, near the same spot that Tao parked just two weeks ago before his "retirement." As he steps out of the Honda, he notices a dark maroon-stained concrete area beneath his feet but fails to make a connection to Tao's bleeding arm. There was no police tape restricting this area, which was never examined by the police, an unusual oversight for the otherwise efficient NYPD detectives. Standing by a brownish red brick wall near the overlook to the Verrazano Bridge, Alex sees Yudansha Greater, who touches his nose as the signal agreed upon at the Goshen Karate Dojo. Alex smiles to himself as he is happy and relieved to see one of his brothers from the kyokai watching his back. As he walks toward Jamieson Hall, he stops a student and asks her where the main library is. The nerdy-looking, glasses-wearing student tells him, "It's that building up on the hill with the four Roman pillars in front. That's the only library on campus."

"Thanks a lot," Alex answers then redirects his stride up the hill and enters the pillared building through a set of glass doors. Right behind him entering the building is Greater, his nebulous cop bodyguard. Ron peruses the area memorizing the faces of the four people currently present in the foyer then sits down at a nearby mahogany table, opens a book but keeping Alex in view.

The librarian, an elderly matron nearly seventy, asks Alex, "May I help you?"

Alex replies, "I'm here to have lunch with Ling."

The woman answers, "Oh, she's in the back. I'll get her for you."

A few minutes later a very slim, more like skinny but very pretty Chinese girl, age thirty-six, walks up to the front desk. She looks like a preppy fourteen-year-old with her angora sweater, conservative length skirt, and wearing booby socks and Weejuns. Alex thinks to himself, *She is actually much prettier than Susan and so collegiate-looking like the girls that I went to college with some twenty-six years ago.* As usual for the species, Ling has a white blouse over her chest that sports no sign of breasts whatsoever.

Alex smiles and says, "Hello, Ling? I'm Al from the ad in the *Star-Ledger*."

"Hello, Al," Ling blurts out shyly. She turns to the elderly matron and says, "Mabel, I am going to have lunch now, okay?"

Mabel responds, "Sure, dear, take your time."

Alex and Ling leave the library followed shortly by Greater.

"Where do you want to have lunch?" Alex asks Ling.

She replies, "Why don't we stay on campus and eat in the school cafeteria?"

Alex agrees as they walk toward Smithson Hall entering on the ground floor. The cafeteria is on the lower level in Smithson connected to the main floor by a spiral staircase with black wrought iron railing. At the end of the self-serve counters is the usual cashier with a balance to weigh the salad bar selections to determine the price. Despite Alex's objections, Ling insists on paying for Alex's lunch as well as her own. They find a nice quiet table near the panoramic windows looking right at the Verrazano. Much small talk is made about likes and dislikes, but Alex senses that he is being interviewed for someone else to date, not for Ling herself. After lunch they get up to walk back to the library when Ling asks Alex to hold her sweater because she has to go to the ladies' room. She shuffles here Weejun-dressed feet sliding and walking toward the bathroom like a little girl. Alex thinks that she is really cute in both looks and mannerisms as he awaits her return. "She seems so sweet," he thinks out loud, "and she's studying the Bible to become a Christian." He also gathered that she is divorced (so what else is new) and has a little seven-year-old daughter named Nanchi back in China. Why isn't her daughter her with her? Is this another Chinese government-sponsored PhD like Shen Tao at Rutgers when he was there?

In any event, Alex is already strongly attracted to Ling despite her lack of a curvy female body and definitely wants to see her again.

Ling returns from the ladies' room, thanks Alex, and takes back her sweater. While the couple walks back to the library, Alex asks, "May I call you again?"

Ling hesitates for a moment then says, "Yes. I need to talk with you more." Ling goes back to work, and Alex leaves Harrison College to also go back to work. Greater waves him goodbye as the two brothers of the kyokai separate on the GSP. Alex gets back to Monochrome at about 2:00 p.m. hardly missed. The picture of Ling plays in his mind over and over like an obsession. He can't believe it—she is prettier than Susan and looks quite conservative, demure, not sleazy like Susan when he first met her. Ling's silky black hair was cut evenly at the base of her slender, kissable neck, sort of a pageboy style. Alex hopes and prays that she will agree to go out with him again; it was kind of left hanging in the air when they parted. He would call her tonight even if that seems a little anxious on his part. After all, he's an anxious guy anyway. Next time he will bring her more chocolates and a long-stemmed red rose and kiss her hand as a greeting gesture. He usually gets to kiss the girl goodbye on the cheek on the first date by asking to do so; he didn't do this with Ling. She seemed so high class, so refined, so proper. Basically he chickened out.

That night as Alex gets home to his Hunterdon log cabin, he tries to stay occupied until 9:00 p.m., the time that he arranged to call Ling. The hesitation in her reply troubled him because he remembered Susan's ever so slight voice and body language change that terminated their relationship. He is basically on a learning expedition with the Chinese girls and wonders if that's the way they dump a guy.

Nine o'clock comes, and Alex tries Ling's number. It's busy. Uh-oh, not another men popular Susan, he hopes. Finally, at nine thirty, he gets through. She says, "I'm sorry. I was talking with my girlfriend, Qing, in Brooklyn. She's very pretty and wants to have a baby right away."

Alex thinks to himself, *Why is she telling me this?*

Then Alex, to avoid another Susan-type rejection, tells Ling about his problem, ED, while he has not gotten fully attached to her yet. She doesn't seem to understand what he is talking about because of a slight language/cultural barrier and because Chinese men rarely have such a problem. That's why there's 2.5 billion Chinese or whatever. There's also an herbal formulation given to men to make them more potent that makes Viagra look like M&Ms with no white chocolate mess. Ling reluctantly agrees to meet Alex again at the college and have dinner with him. He will take her to a Korean Japanese restaurant in Fort Lee, NJ, since she mentioned that she likes Korean food somewhere along the line.

Alex leaves Clark around 4:00 p.m. allowing an additional forty-five minutes for traffic delays on the Goethals and for merging into traffic in Staten Island going toward the other four boroughs of NYC. He picks up Ling at the library giving her a small box of chocolates and a long single-stemmed red rose when she gets into his Honda. As he leaves the parking lot, Yudansha Ed continues to follow him; Ed started watching his back as soon as Alex left the Monochrome building in Clark.

Alex drives across the Goethals back into NJ and gets on the GSP, which is, at rush hour, bumper to bumper. Ling is a little nervous now since she is not a driver and unfamiliar with NJ as well as unfamiliar with Alex; he might reverse the tables on her by being a crazed serial killer for all she knows. She is sitting on the very edge of the gray velour passenger side bucket seat fidgeting.

Finally the traffic breaks after the usual tollbooth backlog, and the couple finally arrives in Fort Lee about 8:00 p.m. Ling has no idea where she is when actually she is only two as the crow flies miles from her graduate school, Columbia.

Alex parks his car in an underground lot under a small shopping mall then opens the door for Ling and escorts her to the elevator. They ride up to the second floor where Furosato's Japanese Korean restaurant is located. Moments later, Yudansha Ed enters the restaurant and takes a nearby table in the hiragana- and katakana-charactered gaily decorated bistro. Unable to decipher just what the food selections are from the menu, Ling plays it safe and orders a noodle dish. Alex, being the more adventurous type, orders something described as beef in the small letter English print under the hira/kata characters. Their meal seems to arrive quickly. Alex sees Ling's noodle dish and tells her to start eating while he waits for his beef dish. Ten minutes go by with no further dishes coming to the table, so he calls the waitress over to their table. "Excuse me, miss? I ordered a beef dish, and it hasn't come yet," Alex tells her. She doesn't seem to understand, so he asks her to bring over the menu again, which she quickly does. Alex points at the selection, which he chose, and the waitress points to a pile of very red thin slices of something on the plate in front of him. He says with surprise, "This is beef?" The waitress assures him that the pile of meat looking very red and raw is the beef dish, which he ordered. He jokingly blurts out, "Beef sushi? Aren't you supposed to cook it?" The chef overhears his comments and says that they can fry it a little bit in a skillet if he would like, but it is usually eaten the way they served it. Alex, quietly embarrassed, tells them that it is fine just the way it is. He takes a mouthful and is now convinced that it is raw meat of some kind, maybe beef, maybe roadkill. Needless to say, he leaves a fair amount untouched and concentrates on filling up on the appetizers while Ling finishes her noodles.

After the couple finishes their meal, Alex pays the check then escorts Ling back to the elevator. He noted that she did not order an alcoholic beverage during dinner—that's good. On the elevator, she starts to talk about an Indian guy (India Indian, not American) whom she went out with describing a situation and asking Alex for the interpretation of this guy's actions. Alex thinks that she is either very naïve about what to discuss on a date or downright rude. *What do I care about some Indian guy who was trying to get into her panties from what I've just heard,* Alex thinks to himself. *Where's the us in this relationship?*

The elevator reaches the lower level, and the couple, if you can call them that, proceeds to the car being carefully observed by kyokai brother Ed who walked down the two flights to stay on watch for Alex's safety. A quick turn of the ignition brings the Honda's four cylinders to life, and Alex takes Ling across the Hudson River via the GWB. Ling immediately begins to recognize where she is; she's near Columbia where she is completing her PhD in library science by writing her final dissertation. After this year, Columbia is terminating the LS PhD program for lack of demand. Most librarians stop at the MLS level and can handle any task required of a librarian without further training.

Ling says, "You can drop me off anywhere in this area since I know it well. I'll walk to my apartment from here." She is still being noncommittal about future dates or a relationship with Alex. Her conversation is very objective, and she apparently doesn't want him to know where she lives either. Alex stops at the curb on W. 168 Street and kisses Ling's hand as she exits the Honda. He watches her walk away in a downtown direction then pulls out into traffic and goes back across the GWB to Jersey. Alex is not seeing any progress in this relationship and feels hurt by Ling's impersonal actions and conversation thus far. The fifty-dollar dinner at the Korean Japanese restaurant was a total waste of money and time. He is really attracted to this preppy China doll, but she has remained aloof so far. At this point, he could only hope that Ling's strange behavior is just a fluke and not a harbinger of what's to follow.

After a few days go by, Alex calls Ling again. As usual, the line is busy. When he gets through, Ling tells him that she was talking to Qing who lives in Brooklyn. Qing is divorced too and is tall for a China doll at 5'7" and very pretty; she looks like a model. Alex again begins to wonder, *Why do I need to know this? My interest is in Ling, not Qing.* Then in a seeming complete turnabout, Ling invites Alex to meet her in Chinatown the next Saturday. She wants to repay him for the Korean Japanese restaurant fiasco by treating him to dim sum. Alex says, "You don't have to repay me. It's a man's obligation to pay during a date." However, Ling insists that she treat him. Alex is confused but happy that he will see Ling again. He has yet to even hold her hand; the more indifferent she seems, the more he wants her like a fire so choked for air that it will draw air like a vacuum cleaner in an attempt to thrive.

18

THE SWITCH: SI CHINA DOLL THROUGH CHINATOWN TO BROOKLYN CHINA DOLL

Alex heads out from Hunterdon to Chinatown, NYC, to meet Ling about 11:00 a.m. that Saturday. He gets there early and parks on the street in front of a no parking sign. Then, before he has walked even a block, he doubles back and reparks his car in a nearby municipal lot. The mental image of the NYPD towing his Honda to an impound lot for parking in a restricted zone motivates him to spend twelve dollars to park his car for two hours. When he gets back to the spot on the street from which he left, another car is parked there surrounded by several more. Although the sign says "No Parking Anytime," those who know Chinatown also know that the NYPD doesn't enforce this rule on Saturdays and Sundays because it's good for business that way. How was Alex supposed to know this?

Standing on the corner of Canal and whatever street, Alex finally spots Ling. He crosses Canal Street to join her. She is wearing khaki shorts and a T-shirt that really accentuates her skinny legs and lack of breasts. But to Alex, she looks beautiful. Ling takes him to one of the bigger Chinese restaurants in Chinatown where dim sum, the equivalent of Sunday dinner for Americans, is proceeding in full swing. They find a table surrounded completely by other tables all full of Chinese people; Alex is just about the only Caucasian there. The procedure, as Alex sees and hears it from Ling, is to stop whatever waiter is serving what you like and ask for as many of those delicacies that you would like to have. The waiter then puts that many on your plate and punches a symbol on your check that you take to the cashier when you're done and pay the going rate for what you ate. All of the delicacies are not priced the same. For example, if you want some Peking duck, that will cost more per serving than a Chinese meatball wrapped in dough. Actually, to Alex, just about everything he tries tastes gamy, which he understands to mean not good or not fresh, filled with the animal toxins that were produced when the animal was traumatized before it was slaughtered. He is developing quite an upset stomach. Alex likes Chinese food, but only the Americanized versions served in non-Chinatowns throughout the USA. He is having another light meal because he doesn't want to tell Ling that this form of Chinese food sucks; she may take that as an insult even if these are the so-called delicacies of the real Chinese culture.

As the couple gets up to leave and pay the check, that is, as Ling insists on paying the check, two more warm oriental bodies plop right into their seats for their "Sunday dinner." Ling tells Alex to wait by the register for a moment while she disappears behind a wall partition apparently to speak to someone she knows. A few minutes later she fetches Alex and introduces him to Qing, the "tall for a China doll" model type woman who wants to have a baby right away. The three walk back to where Alex has his car parked, and he hands the parking attendant the ticket stub locating his car to a valet. In a squealing of tires and a flash of time, the dark blue Honda is in front of them. Alex tips the valet and opens the doors for the ladies. As he leaves the parking lot, Ling in the back seat asks him to drive uptown toward Columbia. When they get there, Ling gets ready to get out as Alex reaches for her hand to kiss her goodbye. She says, "No, no, no," and then yanks her hand out of his hand. She says goodbye and walks away from the car down the street as Alex sits in his car at the curb with Qing in the front passenger seat trying to figure out what just happened.

He says, "Where is she going?" Then turning to Qing, he says, "I don't understand what's going on. You seem like a nice girl, but I thought I had a date with Ling. Where do you live? I'll take you home."

Qing tells him, "I live in an apartment on East 14th street off Avenue X in Brooklyn."

"Qing, I don't know how to get to Brooklyn from here. Can you give me some directions?"

"I don't drive and always take the subway, so I don't know where we are or how to get to Brooklyn by car."

Alex thinks to himself, *That lousy bitch tricked me into a fix-up with Qing. I am going to chew her ass out for this.* Fuming like a bottle of sulfuric acid with sulfur trioxide in it, he drives in the general direction of Brooklyn. Alex now realizes what Ling has done to him over the last several weeks. He's been dumped on Qing, and all the small talk was an interview to see if Alex was to be mated to Qing, not to the interviewer, Ling. Going with the flow, he asks Qing to write her phone number, for lack of a better place, on the map of NYC he is using to figure out where Qing lives so that he can drop her off. She offers to get out and take the subway from Manhattan, but Alex won't allow that; his gentlemanly nature necessitates that he take her to her doorstep even if it takes all day to find it. After about four hours of traveling, crossing the Brooklyn Bridge three times, and countless curbside requests for instructions, he finally gets to East 14th Street.

"You seem like a nice lady, Qing. May I call you?" Alex asks.

Qing's reply is short and sweet, "Of course." Qing leaves the Honda and walks up the sidewalk to her ground-floor apartment.

Alex waits to see that she is able to get inside, waves, then heads down East 14th towards Avenue Y. By trial and error, he finds the signs for the Verrazano, pays the seven-dollar toll, and crosses into Staten Island. From here he knows the route back to his home since it partly retraces the path to NJ from Harrison College on SI. He gets home around 8:00 p.m. thanks to Ling's trickery and getting lost in three of the five boroughs of NYC for five hours. About one minute behind him is Sensei Thomas pulling in to his driveway; he has been on his tail since Chinatown. Alex gets out of his car and apologizes to Sensei for the runaround. Soft-spoken Sensei Thomas looks at him and says, "No problem. Anytime you need backup and I'm free, you got it. Neither the kyokai nor I will allow some misguided Chinese conspiracy end up hurting a brother. I'll go inside with you to check out the house then I'll split. Sensei said "conspiracy." Alex thinks, *It's strange that he should use that particular word. That's exactly what I am starting to think about this whole business. Looks like he is ahead of me in thinking about another situation, as usual. He has a way of knowing these things before anyone else.*

Alex is grateful without limit to Sensei and the kyokai as Thomas heads his Porsche Boxster back toward Hawthorne. Thomas is a sixth degree black belt plus ex-detective for the Dade County Police in Florida. Alex has seen him fight six first degree black belts all at once, and when the smoke clears, Sensei is the only one still standing. He is an outstanding fighter, teacher, and all-around excellent person in every respect. People respect him not out fear but out of admiration.

Despite Alex's building animosity toward Ling, he still longs to hold her, touch her, be with her, and make love with her when he can.

19

THE THREE-HUNDRED-MILE DATE WITH THE BROOKLYN CHINA DOLL

A week goes by as Alex holds off calling either Qing or Ling. He decides to call Qing and ask her about Ling and her seemingly crazy behavior. He dials her phone number written on the map across 34th Street, Manhattan. Her line is busy. "What is it with these women, always on the phone!" he thinks out loud. A few minutes later he presses the redial button. Her line is ringing now. "*Wei?*" comes through the receiver on the other end.

"Hello, Qing? Is this Qing?" he says.

Qing answers, "Yes, who is this?"

"It's Alex from last Saturday, remember?"

"Yes, I remember. How are you?"

"Okay. I wanted to talk with you about Ling for a few minutes."

"Oh, I was just talking with her. She said that you might call."

Kind of presumptuous, Alex thinks.

"What she did last Saturday was very rude. She should call me and apologize," remarks Alex, the idealistic dreamer.

Qing replies, "She's not interested in you. She says she thinks you are ugly. She wants a much younger man."

"What!" Alex says then drops the receiver. He picks it up and continues, "Sorry for that crash. I dropped the phone. She says I'm ugly?"

Qing continues, "Yes. She also says that you're not good for her because she wants to have lots of sex and you have some problem with this."

A fine budding Christian, Alex thinks. *She wants to have a lot of unmarried sex known in any Bible she could possibly be studying as fornication or adultery since she is divorced. Just what the Christian community needs—another lip-service Christian. Alas! Alex, you shouldn't think this way. Remember, "Let him who has no sins cast the first stone," and that sure as hell isn't you. A few months ago you were just about ready to sell your soul to be able to successfully do it with Susan.*

"Listen, Qing. Can I call you back in a few days? I have some work that I must get done right now. Okay?"

Qing replies, "Yes. Please call me back. Goodbye."

Alex replaces the black telephone in its battery-charging cradle. Heavy depression set in as he contemplates what Qing said that Ling said about him. He already was a little in love with Ling even though he may have spent only a total of ten hours with her; this is the Alex pedestal syndrome. It hurt to be rejected, again, by his pedestal oriental potential bride.

A few more days go by, and he decides that it's time to pull himself up by the bootstraps and get back in the game. Qing is a very attractive woman, so why not try her? He decides to call her to set up a date for the coming weekend. These girls are getting further and further away from his home base. First, Susan in Nutley, about forty miles; second, Ling in Staten Island, about fifty-five miles; now,

Qing in Brooklyn, close to sixty-five miles. Same for the expenses: gas for forty miles one way, gas for fifty-five miles and a four-dollar toll, and gas for sixty-five miles plus a four-dollar toll going and a seven-dollar toll returning on the Verrazano. Of course Alex could take the Brooklyn Bridge then one of the tunnels back and save the seven dollars, but it means losing one hour getting stuck in cross Manhattan traffic.

"*Wei*," Qing answers her phone.

"Hi, Qing, this is Alex. Ni hao ma? (How are you?)"

Qing replies, "Ni hao, xiexie. You can speak Chinese?"

Alex replies "Yes. You have just heard all that I know. I was wondering if you would like to go to the Jersey Shore this Saturday."

Qing is delighted. "Yes. I would like that very much. When will you pick me up? I don't drive."

Alex replies, "I know. Can you be ready about 10:00 a.m.? Because it's a pretty long drive." Boy, that's an understatement. This date would ultimately put three hundred miles on the Honda's odometer.

Qing agrees to be ready by 10:00 a.m. next Saturday. Alex says, "Xiexie (thank you)," and Qing replies with something like "You're welcome" in Mandarin. Qing works in Manhattan as a word processor for a small Chinese import-export company. She is paid roughly three hundred dollars per week before taxes and pays five hundred dollars/month for rent in her Sheep Head's Bay area apartment off Avenue X. This area of Brooklyn is mostly row houses and inhabited by newly immigrated Chinese and Russians plus innumerous other ethnic groups. The neighborhood is more or less a safe one, but one would be advised to put the "club" on your steering wheel because cars do disappear from here regularly.

Alex brings some Hagstrom maps of NYC with its five boroughs. He charts a course to East 14th Street from his Hunterdon cabin in NJ. Not allowing for construction, roadblocks, detours, and one-way streets (of which Brooklyn is loaded with), he figures that it will take 1.5 hours plus or minus two hours depending on prevalent road conditions to get to Qing's apartment.

Saturday at 8:00 a.m. Alex shoves a handful of pills in his mouth, washes them down with orange juice, then leaves for Brooklyn. This time he is not using the motorcycle since Qing is likely to balk at the idea of her riding on the tiny plateau of a passenger seat with a six-inch sissy bar supporting her back. The trip is uneventful, and he meets Qing at 9:45 a.m. She is wearing a beige full ankle-length dress with pastel flowers of pink, lime, and yellow on it (wouldn't that look great on a motorcycle!). Of course the dress is buttoned to the top of her slender neck to a choke like collar. She looks very conservative and extremely beautiful. Her 5'7" stature at a slim 110 lbs. enhances her model-like appearance. There are no bumps under her dress top at all, not even a hint of a small hill. Alex has bigger breasts than her. She is the Chinese equivalent of Olive Oil, Popeye's girlfriend.

As they leave Brooklyn across the Verrazano toward Staten Island, Yudansha (high degree black belt) "Vincent" Meng Ho follows in his Oldsmobile 442. Meng is a Taiwanese who lived in the Kowloon Bay area near Hong Kong before he came to graduate school in New Jersey where he met Alex. Meng's research lab was across the hall from Alex's on the second floor of the Wright Reedman chemistry building. Meng practiced tai chi chuan and kung fu, two indigenous Chinese forms of martial arts. Between experiments, the two friends would do mock kumite (sparring) in the back of Ho's lab. Vincent (the English equivalent of Meng, so he says) was a very good friend of Alex teaching him some kung fu and that ABC girl means "American-Born Chinese." He hated the Japanese and the Communist Chinese because of what they did to his family during WWII. Several of his brothers were killed by these barbarians. In fact, his parents lost so many children in the war that they later decided to have more children; Meng was their tenth child and may not have been conceived had his brothers survived the war.

With Ming in his 442 was his girlfriend, Lourdes, a Filipina he met while teaching freshman chemistry labs at the state university. When the two couples, Meng and Lourdes and Alex and Qing, get to the shore, they will be in close proximity but will not greet each other; just two independent couples walking on the boardwalk while Vincent watches Alex's back. Vincent, at 5'6" and 130 lbs., is much smaller than Alex and actually shorter than Qing. But he is lightning fast in his kung fu techniques being the modern-day equivalent of a Shaolin priest including the fire branded dragon and tiger on his forearms. With his thick black-rimmed glasses, he looks like a Chinese Woody Allen, very nerdy and not at all the master of the martial arts. He has frequently trained with Alex in Hawthorne at Sensei Thomas's Dojo.

Qing is fairly quiet on the trip and seems to be very much at ease with Alex. She has two advantages over the other China dolls: her quota is only one high-quality American per six months since she is Ping's niece, and her finely tuned body, a product of her gym workouts, can be positioned in many gymnastic ways making her very sexually stimulating even without large breasts to play with. She, like many other Chinese women, did not lactate from her oversized nipples mounted on a nearly flat chest. Her strategy is to coerce her victims into intercourse under the guise of wanting desperately to have a baby since, at thirty-eight, her biological clock is winding down.

After about two hours, Alex and Qing arrive at Seaside Heights, NJ. It's a pleasant sunny day with the temperature around 75°F. A cool, tropical-like breeze is coming off the ocean to add to the day's pleasantness. Since the summer season hasn't arrived yet, there are only handfuls of people on the boardwalk. As the couple walks along individually, not yet hand in hand, Alex ducks into gaming parlors frequently to maneuver a stuffed animal out of a claw machine. Some claws have little rubber grips on one or more of their three prongs; other claw machines have obtainable stuffed animals not jammed tightly between others and easy to extract. Alex is a claw-reading and manipulating expert having obtained (for a large number of quarters) over one hundred stuffed animals in his claw career given to the New Yorka ex-girlfriend who spitefully drove to his house and dumped them in his driveway after the breakup. That action just reaffirmed the appropriateness of his breaking up with her; it didn't create guilt in Alex as she had thought it would. Why not keep the stuffed animals and give back the sewing machine, food processor, and engagement ring? A strange woman's logic, to be sure, operated here.

Qing, by this time, now has an armful of stuffed animals as Alex pounds the frog jump launching the rubber frog skyward and landing it dead center in a floating green-and-yellow flower petal. Bingo!

Another stuffed animal is awarded to Qing for his success. As Qing is receiving the latest two-tone green dinosaur, Vincent and Lourdes walk by stopping just feet away to look at the ocean for a moment. Alex winks at Vincent who touches his nose as a return confirmation gesture.

After a feast of typical seashore junk food that will spend the next two hours irritating the stomach walls, the couple heads back to the car parked on a sand and stone side street. The meter still has one hour of purchased parking time on it, but Alex has become bored with the entire scenario and decides that they're leaving. It is a two-hour drive to Brooklyn then two more hours to Hunterdon.

As they ride home, Alex seizes the opportunity to explain to Qing his ED problem. Unsurprisingly she doesn't seem to understand what he is talking about since this doesn't happen to Chinese guys; they invented sex and forced it on any and all women willing or not, unable to run away in their undersized shoes they were forced to wear. With Qing's build, she could do a four-minute mile. But she's not running away from sex; she's running toward it—she wants to have a baby.

20

CHINATOWN ESCAPADE IN ED

Saturday morning, the best time of the week, has finally arrived. Today's agenda: go to Brooklyn and pick up Qing then drive to Chinatown to see an herbalist doctor with no degree.

Alex rolls out of bed about nine thirty and, as usual, shaves, gets dressed, skips breakfast except for the OJ, and is on the road at nine forty. He's on his own today since all his bros are competing in a tournament today.

Another nice mid-summer day in Hunterdon erodes with time as he gets closer and closer to NYC. Smelly garbage dump Staten Island is particularly foul today due to the heat and unrelenting humidity. The Verrazano traffic is light for this time of day and year, and before you know it, he is across and hip deep in the Belt Parkway traffic logjam. Looks like everybody's going to the Long Island beaches today.

He reaches the exit for Coney Island, a few quick turns and voila! X Avenue, Brooklyn, USA. He rights onto Avenue X, two blocks then right on to E 14th Street. Fifty yards down on the right is Qing's apartment.

Confronting the perennial problem in New York's five boroughs—finding a parking space that doesn't block someone's driveway or is not situated in front of a fireplug—he wonders how this never seems to bother most New Yorkers. It bothers him because he has NJ plates and doesn't know the way to the impound lot by subway. Ahh, there's a space and only two blocks away from Qing's apartment. On goes the club and out goes Alex for the two looooong city block trek. Finally, 2.5 hours after leaving Hunterdon, he's at Qing's apartment and exactly at noon.

He knocks on the glass of the door. She comes to the door and opens it. "Hi, come in. I'm almost ready." Isn't that an oxymoron for a woman, "almost ready"?

"Hi, Qing, you look very nice today, like a model," Alex states a near fact. She is tall and slender and flexible. She's dressed in a dungaree suit, jeans, and jacket. Qing has a red ribbon tied around her neck like a choke collar. Her shiny, silky black hair and dark eyes contrast beautifully with that touch of red. She is truly a beautiful woman by anyone's standards. She is, however, a little self-conscious about her 5'7" height and tends to stoop a little.

"Would you like something to drink?" she inquires. Alex politely accepts her offer of a nonalcoholic beverage and sits down on the kitchen table which is sort of in the kitchen but also in the parlor in her three-room apartment. The kitchen is the parlor and vice versa depending on whether you're eating or not. At the rear of the kitchen-parlor is a window with bars on it. The apartment is on the ground floor, so the Chinese landlord who extracts five hundred dollars/month from her added a little extra security.

Qing and Alex exit the apartment as he says, "Wait here and I'll pick you up. My car is two blocks away." He jogs up East 14th Street to the Honda, opens it, unlocks the club, starts it up, and leaves his precious space which already has two cars hovering over it. He starts to sing, "Start spreading the news. I'm leaving today. I want to be a part of it, New York, New York." His sarcasm brings a smile to his face. *Like I really want to be in New York, home of all the modern amusements one could desire. There are drugs, prostitution, homicide, street gangs, assassinations, plus anything else your little heart* *desires. The entrance fee at the gate of this zoo is $4.00 from New Jersey; $2.00—no, 2.50; no, 2.75; no, 3.00; no, 3.50 from the TBTA ports of entry. Even though inflation is only 4 percent, bridge and tunnel tolls run a 20 percent rate. The JBTA's logic is that the tolls must be raised is reduce the traffic into the city. Then when drivers diminish, the tolls have to be raised to cover expenses which are not being met due to the reduced traffic. Either way, you lose.*

The dark blue Honda comes to a stop right alongside Qing's driveway which isn't her driveway since she doesn't drive and doesn't have a vehicle. The power door locks click open, and Qing gets in. The couple heads toward the Brooklyn Bridge to get to lower Manhattan, specifically Chinatown. By divine intervention, Alex finds a parking space only three blocks from Qing's Chinese "doctor" that is going to cure his ED. Now he will be able to be infected by Qing, i.e., so that he can impregnate her. Yes, he is tired of hearing the litany "I want to have a baby." He is willing to try anything to get inside her and give her what she wants. What a gentleman, what a bleeding heart, what a soft-headed chump! Always trying his best to give his girl whatever she wants, even this! Women claim that they would love to find a sensitive, thoughtful guy like this. So why isn't Alex married already? It's a long, looong story; women aren't always logical and aren't satisfied when you give them what you thought they wanted. Their meaning is in their body language, not their words. But God bless them because they bring the beauty to a man's world of hard, cold, and calculating logic. He didn't' understand this well until he finally got married, but not to Qing.

Qing and Alex walk up a flight of stairs above a Peking duck grocery store. This is where Mr. Chu, herbalist-acupuncturist "doctor," has his office. As they arrive on the second-floor landing, a glass countertop set of display cases is center stage. In there are all kinds of herbs, spices, and animal parts. There is elk horn and hoof, rhinoceros nose horn, dried scorpions, etc. ground up into magical powders. A Chinese lady acting as a receptionist asks the couple, "May I help you?" Qing rattles off a large packet of Mandarin words, sentences, and the lady tries to conceal the smirk on her face. Alex surmises the reason for the smirk and is mildly embarrassed like when you go to enter the men's room and a woman walks out. You think that you entered the wrong door until her badged gray uniform announces her cleaning lady role. His face starts to redden, reaches pink, then subsides back to its normal Caucasian off-white.

The receptionist goes into another room to alert the "doctor." He is a middle-aged Chinese man dressed in a brown suit sitting at his desk. She bids them to enter the room and sit down. The "doctor" extends his arm for a handshake then motions for them to be seated. Mr. Chu says, "What is your problem?"

Alex thinks, *The problem is that I want to get laid by this gorgeous gal with me, but I can't get it up when I'm with her*. However, that's not what comes out of his mouth. He starts to explain, but Qing interrupts by spewing out some more Mandarin causing Chu to smirk.

He says to Alex, "So it no go up for you."

Alex thinks, *Hey, Chu, don't bullshit around, just go right to the bottom line. Thanks a lot, pal.* His face is now the color of a red delicious apple with a little blotch of Caucasian pink/off-white.

Chu says, "No big deal. I have special herbal cure for this problem. Three-month supply for four hundred dollars."

Alex thinks, *Are you out of your fucking mind? This guy's a snake oil medicine doctor out of the 1800s in the Wild West.* Finally Alex says, "I can't afford to spend four hundred dollars on something that may or may not work."

Chu answers, "Insurance will pay for it. I'll write down it's for acupuncture. Most insurance plans cover acupuncture treatment. Maybe we'll do some acupuncture later if it still no go up."

Alex is not exactly a virgin when it comes to medical scams, but boy, this guy shows no fear at all about defrauding an insurance company. He thinks, *Suppose I was a secret agent for an insurance company, Chu would be dead in the water. He is running quite a scam here, but then again, maybe he does have a way to make it "go up." After all, aren't there nearly two billion Chinese? All those stiff dicks looking around for something to screw—how barbaric! Maybe I should just punch this guy out and save America from another charlatan. But if I do that, Qing might be just a little bit angry since this is her idea in the first place.*

Alex says, "My insurance company doesn't cover very much and probably not acupuncture. Maybe I can try it for just one month. How much for a one-month supply?"

Chu says, "One hundred twenty-five dollar for one month."

Alex thinks, *What the hell kind of math is that? Doesn't three times one hundred twenty-five equal three hundred seventy-five, not four hundred? Do I get green stamps with the four-hundred-dollar supply? Or maybe Chu throws in a hooker to see if the cure took after three months.*

Chu says, "We take credit card—Master card, Visa card, American Express card, no problem."

No problem? Alex thinks. *What if I plant my foot up your ass, Chu, will that be a problem?* Qing looks at him with her deep, dark bedroom eyes like a stray little puppy, and Alex melts. "Okay, I'll try your remedy for one month. Here, it's my Visa card."

The receptionist takes it and writes out a charge bill: One hundred twenty-five dollars plus fifteen-dollar consulting fee plus NYC 81/4 percent tax, total one hundred fifty-two dollars. She hands it back to Alex as he looks at the one-hundred-fifty-two-dollar charge with growing anger. He thinks, *I'm going to blend this guy into that red Chinese tapestry over there.* But on second thought, he says nothing as he looks at Qing's puppy dog eyes. He signs the bill and gets a receipt.

Chu asks him to wait in the first room while his receptionist blends the right ingredients that Chu scribbled in kanji on a prescription-like form. A little bit of this, a little bit of that using "great" weighing precision using a handheld lever-type scale. A mere forty-five minutes later, she hands Alex a small plastic bag with a medium brown powder in it. He is to mix two teaspoons of what looks like powdered feces with one cup of warm water and drink it four times a day. After four weeks, he is to call Mr. Chu to discuss the results, viz: is it up or what?

Alex doesn't realize how close his thinking is to the truth. Not only is this guy a quack, he's a top operative in Ping's satanic conspiracy. Chu prescribed a sweet-smelling mixture of herbs laced with an ergot alkaloid, strychnine, as a cure for his ED. Strychnine is a powerful poison; in fact, so powerful that it takes only a few milligrams to kill a guy as big as Alex. Over the next month he will be getting sicker and sicker until the end. This was a direct order from Ping to Qing and Chu. Retire this resilient sob with extreme prejudice. A naive, compassionate guy trying to make Qing happy was targeted for extinction. How could Qing do this to him? The incentive was the safety of her ailing Russian grandmother locked in a Tibetan reform camp.

The couple leaves the herbal pharmacy and finds a local restaurant for lunch. All the while that they are in Chinatown, Qing does not hold Alex's hand. They are strangers.

After lunch Qing insists on stopping in a Buddhist temple nearby. She takes Alex in, and he sits down on a wooden backless bench. She lights some wooden sticks and places them in a sand-filled bucket, while she seems to be whispering her prayers and requests. The temple is very ornate with gold and red Chinese figures and symbols everywhere. At the exit there is a monk who quietly solicits donations to maintain the facility. As they leave the temple, he begins to understand why Chinese women are so "easy." There is nothing in their religious beliefs that prohibits them from sexual intercourse with anybody at any time. Unlike the Christian guilt trip—mortal sin—their culture would be called by a Westerner indiscriminate or even promiscuous demeanor. These thoughts stir up the potent left over nineteen-year-old Alex causing his groin vain to pulse wildly. He can visualize Qing mounted on top of him receiving his semen to procreate her baby. This excites him, but you just can't have sex on a crowded street in Chinatown on the hood of a Chevrolet in broad daylight. Johnson backs off returning to his flaccid comatose state.

Qing decides to walk into an herbal pharmacy and tea shop. She purchases some ground tea leaves of lavender. Alex is a curiosity in the shop being observed and surrounded by many exotic, almond-eyed and silky black-haired young Chinese women. He feels an attraction to each of them, thinking, *Okay, ladies, now that I'm potent, line up, drop your panties, and bend over with your hands on the counters. I'm going to impregnate every one of you three or four times each*. Wow, a powerful imagination this scientist has! And a dirty mind too!

Hearing Qing's voice, "Let's go," snaps him back to reality, a reality devoid of any real sexual activity. But things are looking up, and soon "it" may go up with the dosages of the precious brown powder. He smiles at Qing as they leave the store. He will start the powder tonight.

21

THE BROWN POWDER ED CURE

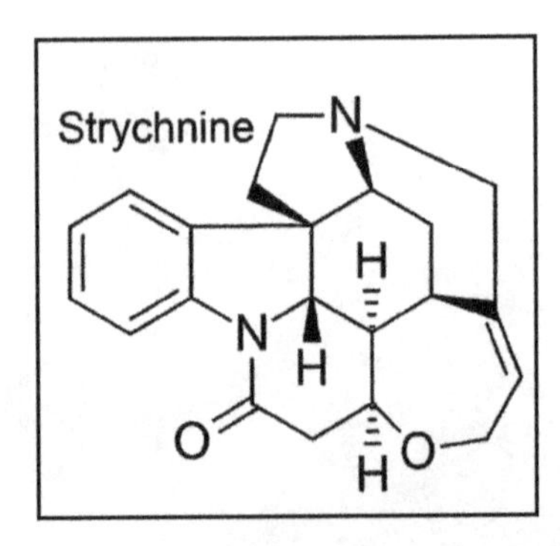

It's late Saturday night when Alex gets back to Hunterdon—too late to brew up some ED cure drink. He needs to sleep well after the day's ludicrous Chinatown experience. It seems more and more ridiculous every day he spends with Qing, or, for that matter, with any of these China dolls. Hooking up on the first date is okay, but kissing on the lips requires being in love. Isn't that backassward in the West?

Sunday morning, eleven o'clock, Alex wakes up and leaps out of bed realizing that the day is being wasted away by lying in bed. Nice headache this morning as he reviews yesterday's events. Breakfast? No thanks. Church? He better go, otherwise he'll face the guilt trip placed there by his Christian upbringing.

Church gets out at 1:30 p.m.—now the day half shot. It's time to brew up some medium brown powder from Chinatown. Two tea-spoonful to a cup of warm water. Up to the face, over the chin—look out, stomach, it's coming in. Yuck! This stuff tastes like lavender tea with a distinct acrid after taste. Alex hates lavender tea. Besides that, the powder doesn't solubilize well in warm water. More bullshit, he suspects.

Slowly, over a period of about three hours, he begins to feel very weak like he used to when he ate Chinese takeout that had tons of MSG. His stomach starts to revolt and cramp. *It must be the burritos that I had for lunch*, he thinks. Time for another dose of the medium brown shit. Up to the face...yada, yada, yada. Yuck! His stomach is doing cartwheels. The powder won't stay down this time. He runs to the toilet and refunds the evil brew depositing it in the wash basin not able to reach the commode. *There's something bad in this powder*, he thought. *It's not the burritos because I've done worse than that. It's this brown powder. Maybe it's interacting with the panic control drug, imipramine. In any event, no more powder until it's analyzed.* But his access to HPLC and MS (high-performance liquid chromatography, mass spectrometry) was lost when he lost his position at 3N Corporation.

He muses, *Maybe Greater can bring this stuff to forensics in Wayne or Hamilton.*

He calls Yudansha Greater. "Ron?"

"Hey, Alex, what's going on?"

"This may sound crazy, but..." Alex explains the details to Ron.

Ron says, "I can give your powder to Sensei Tom Van deGraff. He has access to the NJ forensic labs in Hamilton because he's a state trooper now. Don't, under any circumstances, ingest any more of that junk until we find out what's in it. Bring it to the dojo Monday night and give it to me."

Alex replies, "Thanks, Ron," then hangs up the receiver. He returns to the bathroom and heaves a little more, but basically the powder drink is no longer with him.

22

MEETING AT THE DOJO

After looking for work all day Monday, Alex drives straight to the dojo in Hawthorne.

"*Osu*," he says as he reis (bows), the customary practice when entering the dojo. Ron is at the front desk logging in the students and securing his police firearm sans the magazine in one drawer and the magazine in a second drawer after removing the shells.

"Did you bring the powder?" he asks Alex.

Alex, looking a little pale, weakly says, "It's right here in this plastic bag. I feel pretty lousy right now. On the ride here, my motorcycle almost got totaled by a tractor trailer."

"Another attempted hit?" Ron injects.

Alex answers, "No. I don't think so. It was my fault since I didn't sleep well last night. I was dozing."

Ron questions, "Dozing on a motorcycle? That's impossible with the whipping wind and cold air. That shit that the Chinatown medicine show doctor gave you must be affecting you."

Tom Van deGraff bows off the mat and enters the foyer. "You look like shit, Alex. Get your gi on so I can wake up your ass or kick it, whatever you're up for."

Ron chimes in, "Give him a break, Tom. Some Chinatown guy may be trying to poison him." These words hit Alex hard, and he now links this brown powder to another attempt on his life. Strangely, though, he fails to see Qing as part of this plot. Love, even like, is truly blind. He decides to wait for the forensic report before he goes back to Chinatown and starts accusing people.

Ron gives Tom the brown powder packet, and Tom puts it in his gym bag. "I'll drop it off tomorrow at the state forensics lab since I'm going to Hamilton tomorrow for a police escort to protect the governor's trip to the new state house opening near Trenton. They'll process it and issue a report in a few hours to me or you with my authorization.

"Thanks, Tom. I'll not mess with any other remedies until we clear this up," Alex replies. He continues, "Give me a rain check on the ass-kicking. I'm going to my folks' home in Fair Lawn and rest out this queasiness. No sense riding the bike fifty-five miles back to Hunterdon in this condition."

Ron says, "Remedies for what, Alex?"

Alex answers, "I'm not going to tell you, and you don't want to know."

Ron and Tom both laugh out loud.

"*Oyasuminasai*," Alex says as he bows out of the dojo. He gets on his VT-1100 and rides the short three miles to his parents' house. He parks the bike in their driveway then walks up the red brick stairs and keys the front door. "Hey, Ma, Dad, surprise visit. I was at the dojo, so I thought I'd check up on you guys. I'm a little tired, so I'm going to crash out in the basement on my old couch."

A few hours later, Alex wakes up with a near migraine. He grabs a bottle of acetaminophen, aka Tylenol, washing down a couple with the rest of a Coke which he left on the arm of the couch. The Coke is flat and at room temperature having been sitting there while he sacked out. Within an hour, his headache has weakened greatly. Alex now feels strengthened and awake enough to ride back to Hunterdon. Of course, Mom and Dad are against this idea and convince him to sleep over. Being the forever obedient son, he takes their advice since it has been consistently good in the past. Scrounging around, he finds some Nathan's hot dogs and fries a couple in their microwave then loads them up with Dijon mustard. The dogs seem to be sitting okay in his stomach. He turns on the boob tube to HBO and an old *Kung Fu* episode is playing. Shaolin Master Po tells grasshopper that things are not always as they appear to be. Po illustrates this by placing the bottom half of his staff in a water pool near the Shaolin temple. The staff appears to be separated into two parts. Alex knows this law of physics well, and it's called refraction. But the "things are not as they appear to be" reverberates in his head. He thinks how true this bit of wisdom is, especially in the last few months. You can't react to what you perceive is happening; you react to what's actually happening. All the homicidal attacks came at me after I started messing with Chinese babes. Maybe if I switch to another Asian nationality like Filipino or Korean, people will stop trying to kill me. This thing with Qing doesn't look promising. *I'll cautiously hang around for a while longer and see what develops.*

Tuesday morning Alex is awakened by the telephone when Dad yells downstairs, "Hey, Alex, it's for you."

Groggily, Alex answers, "Hello, this is Alex."

The voice on the other line says, "Trooper Van deGraff asked us to call Dr. Supenski and give him a report of the analysis of a medium brown powder."

Alex says, "This is Dr. Alex Supenski speaking."

The voice continues, "The substance contains mostly harmless herbs indigenous to southern China. Our first tests didn't show any narcotics or other DEA controlled substances. However, our forensic alkaloid expert, Dr. Stan Mazzo, ran a sample through our Hewlett/Packard HPLC then fed the separated chemicals into a mass spectrometer. He found 0.05 percent [m/m] of the chemical strychnine in the mix. This is a very powerful poison that has an acrid taste even at this very low concentration. It could kill a person quickly if the dose was large enough. At lower dosages, it tends to accumulate in the kidneys causing renal failure if continually ingested. Also, over the course of a month, some clinical tests with laboratory rats caused them to die due to cardiac arrest."

Alex is infuriated. Holding back his murderous temper, he says, "Thanks, guys, and thank Trooper Tom V. for me too. I know what I must do now," then hangs up the phone. Mr. Chu is about to get an unannounced visit.

He calls his good friend from graduate school, Vincent Ming Ho, and asks him to meet him in Chinatown on the corner of Canal and Mott Streets in about two hours. Ho speaks four dialects of Chinese besides English, Japanese, and Tagalog (Philippines). Vincent, after hearing the story, is really pissed and offers to give Chu a lesson in pain that he will not soon forget. Alex convinces him that he himself must give him the lesson.

23

REVENGEFUL REVISIT TO CHINATOWN

At noon, New York City, Chinatown, the boys meet at the corner of Canal and Mott Streets. Alex and Ming walk to the building entrance of the acupuncturist Chu. Upon arriving on the second floor, Chu's receptionist yells something in Mandarin then tries to run out of the room. Ho grabs her, tells her to be quiet, and sits her down on her chair. Chu opens his bamboo office door, sees Alex, then slams the door shut. He goes to his desk drawer, pulls out a .25 caliber Berretta, and fires five shots through the door in a fit of panic. Ho and Alex are not hit and wait on the other side of the door. After Ho escorts Chu's receptionist downstairs with his hand over her mouth, Alex is left alone waiting at the doorjamb. Nothing happens for about ten minutes. Then Chu opens the door slowly, gun in hand. Suddenly he sees Alex, so he points the gun at him and pulls the trigger twice. *Click, click.* No more bullets in the five-round magazine. Chu quickly reaches into his pocket for another full magazine. But before he can reload, Alex is on him like flies on dog shit. He grabs Chu's pistol-bearing arm, stoops down, and brings the arm over his right shoulder and pulls down. A loud crack is heard as the arm breaks at the elbow. Chu drops his weapon and cries out in pain. Alex then takes Chu by the collar and places a focused fist to Chu's nose causing it break apart like uncooked spaghetti being cracked into several pieces. Chu is bleeding profusely, and his face is covered with blood and pieces of nose cartilage. Alex throws Chu over his desk landing him in his chair. He delivers a short, bleak message: "Next time I come here, you better be gone, or I'll terminate your ass if you're not. And tell your associates that they are up against one of the most powerful karate kyokais in the United States. If they want to continue to stalk me, a lot of your people are going to get dead, including whomever is master minding this conspiracy."

Chu, bloodied and frightened beyond control, instantly loses the contents of his bladder, soaking himself in urine. Alex gives him the finger and leaves quietly. He meets Ho downstairs, and the two head over to midtown Manhattan where Qing is employed: 65 Park Ave, tenth floor—Chan's Import-Export Association Incorporated LLC. The boys take the elevator to the ninth floor to remove the possibility of encountering some undesirables. As they climb the final steps to the tenth floor, they see a husky, well-developed man guarding the door to the entrance of Qing's work area. Ho politely asks him to step aside in Mandarin. The guard doesn't move. Ho asks the man once more to step aside and identifies himself as a Shaolin priest showing a tiger on one forearm and a dragon on the other. Ho is a founding member of the Red Dragon Kung Fu Association. The guard laughs at him and curses his association calling it a group of pussies (in Mandarin). Ho reacts like a biker who has just had his colors rat-fucked. He delivers a single blow to the guard's muscle-bound abdomen. The guard doubles up and drops to the floor clutching his stomach and coughing up blood.

Alex looks at Ho and says, "Very impressive, Ming."

The two brothers in arms open the door and walk up to Qing's work station. She is pounding the keyboard when she sees Alex. "What are you doing here?" she asks.

Alex tells her about the poison that Chu prescribed and is on the verge of hitting a woman for the first time in his life. Qing starts to cry and tells him that she knows nothing of Chu's business involvements. She thought he was a legitimate Chinese herbalist doctor. Soft-hearted Alex pulls her to him and hugs her. He says, "It's okay, Qing. I believe you." Qing holds him tightly against her body, and he and Johnson begin to get aroused. *Damn it*, he thinks, *I can't have sex with her in this office in front of several people and Ho.*

Her boss comes over to her work station and asks her in Mandarin what the problem is. Ho answers, "No problem, we were just leaving," motioning to Alex to go. Her boss follows them to the exit then sees his burly guard sprawled out on the floor gagging on his own blood. Ho and Alex get into the elevator and make a quick exit out of the building and out of New York City.

24

ANOTHER ATTEMPT ON ALEX'S LIFE WITHOUT QING

A few weeks pass, and the Qing-Alex relationship is heading nowhere. Alex, recently unemployed, unilaterally decides to end this pointless exercise with her. He's been spending money on a woman who wants to have a baby but has yet to kiss him on the lips. He stops calling her, and soon she stops calling him. Then one day at the end of the summer, she calls him and tells him that's she's pregnant. Qing actually expects that he should be elated that she has successfully infected another guy and simultaneously got pregnant. Alex doesn't share her "good news" and figures that after two months she went out with another guy and had sex with him during fertility. Alex tells her that she belongs to this new gentleman, and he has no further interest in her. How could he after hearing of her success with another man?

By a strange but somewhat expected coincidence, within a week of her last phone call, another assassination attempt is tried on him.

He is riding back to Hunterdon on his Honda Shadow one evening after karate class in Hawthorne. Ming is about one hundred feet behind him in his Olds 442. As Alex signals to turn right onto route 78W from 287S near Bridgewater, a light brown Ford Taurus cuts off several cars and is on his tail. The Taurus crosses the rumble strip to pass Alex on the right then suddenly veers sharply to the left attempting to run him off the road into the trees covering the median hill. He sees the car at the right veer and instantly slams on the brakes smoking the rear tire. As the Taurus passes him and hits one of the trees on the median, he accelerates hard to leave it in his dust. Unfazed, the Taurus driver, with a shattered driver's side headlight and crumpled fender, gets back on the road and attempts to catch up to him. Alex rolls the throttle on the big twin and disappears up the road. Ho, in his 442, had been momentarily separated from Alex by the reckless action of the Taurus at the 78W–287S junction. The Taurus catches up to Alex and is almost on his tail. Ho, in the middle lane, overtakes the Taurus with his big 442 V-8. He powers down the passenger side window and throws a five-pound box of roofing nails into the path of the Taurus. Seconds later the Taurus spins out of control ending up on the median between west and east Route 78.

Meanwhile, Alex has positioned his bike between two tractor trailers (in the rocking chair) becoming invisible to the traffic behind him. He gets off at the Oldwick exit and takes the back roads to his cabin. Ho pulls in his driveway seconds after him. Alex goes into his house and retrieves two 9mm Glock 19s.

Giving one to Ho, Alex and Ho get into Alex's truck. They return to the scene of the crime on route 78E. When the two brothers locate the Taurus that spun off the road, the car is abandoned with no sign of any occupants. Alex copies the license plate numbers from the light brown Taurus with its pulverized headlight and crumpled fender. The car also has three flat tires with protruding roofing nails.

Ho and Alex go back to Alex's house and relay the plate number to Ron Greater, the Bergen County cop. The car turns out to be recently stolen from the Chinatown impound lot. Now the kyokai knows that Alex is in real danger. From this moment, the karate/kung fu brothers assign a twenty-four-hour guard to Alex until the death threats cease.

25

HUNTERDON TO HAWTHORNE: STRATEGY OF THE BLACK BELTS

It's an autumnal-like sunny Thursday morning. Alex has been up most of the night still shaken up by the last assassination attempt. After the adrenalin rush came the anxiety rush, almost like taking cocaine then crashing later. Realizing that any more attempts to fall asleep were useless, he gets out of bed and finds Ho already up and doing his tai chi and kung fu exercises out on the back deck. Alex's nerves are quieted by the calm confidence of Ho as he works out. He watches Ho for a few minutes, but Ho is unaware of his presence being totally into his kata. Ho completes his exercise and assumes the lotus position for meditation. Full lotus with legs crossed and heels on thighs, back straight, eyes closed, and arms resting on his knees with the fingers of each hand carving out a smooth circle that looks like the American A-OK sign.

Greater pulls into the driveway with his dark blue Durango. He's dressed in a blue jogging suit with a gold stripe running the length of his pants on each side. He has already jogged the five miles to town and back along the south branch of the Raritan River that traverses the Ken Lockwood Gorge. He isn't even winded when he walks onto the deck to begin his own set of karate exercises.

Ho returns to normal consciousness as Greater bows and says, "*Osu, Sifu*," a term of high respect for Ho. Ho returns the gestures. Ron yells, "Hey, Alex, you lazy bum. Get your ass out here and lose some of the middle-aged fat. C'mon, *hayaku* (hurry up)."

"Not today, guys, chill out," Alex remarks.

Ron taunts him "Nidansha, Dai Nihon Ten no Kata now!" Realizing that he can't worm his way out of exercising any longer, Alex, in his skivvies, walks out onto the deck, reis (bows), and begins Dai Nihon Ten no Kata. Greater observes the precision of each move saying nothing. Alex is rusty from years of neglect, but half-way through the exercise, he becomes focused and razor-sharp. He completes the set and returns to the ready position (hachiji dachi). Greater chides him, "Not bad on the back half for an old man."

Alex interjects, "Gichin Funakoshi was at his best form at the ripe old age of eighty-eight, I believe."

Greater says, "Touché."

The three brothers exercise for another hour then take turns in the bone-chilling shower.

Ron says, "Got to look sharp in the dojo. Big boss from Okinawa is in town this morning." He was referring to Hanshi Lenten, the Marine Corps lifer that was stationed in Okinawa for twelve years. He studied under several masters there and got their permission to combine their six different systems into one called Cajun Goshen Do. This is the system that is practiced by Greater, Alex, and Sensei Thomas and many others. Ho knew much of this modified Goshen Do but was primarily a kung fu practitioner.

The three brothers in combat get into Greater's Durango and leave for Hawthorne. Greater is at this time an off-duty cop, so he has his Smith & Wesson 9mm handgun with him. Alex feels secure with two of his long-term associates watching his back. Ron is pushing 90 mph going east on Route 78 then 287 north then 80 east only slowing down for the highway changes. A state trooper with red, white, and blue lights flashing pulls alongside the Durango, sees Greater's PBA medallion, and signals him through with a thumbs-up. The boys reach the dojo in a record forty-five minutes.

Gym bags with protective equipment, karate gis (uniforms), and black belts in hand, the three enter the training hall at 9:30 a.m. Greater takes his pistol, separates the magazine from it, pulls the slide to eject the shell in the chamber, peels the shells out of the magazine, then hands all to Sensei Thomas who locks these three items in three different drawers, locking each one and giving the key to Ron.

The students present are all different levels of black belts with Sensei being the highest at sixth dan. His belt is black with a red stripe running up the center of the belt. But today, he is outranked by Hanshi Lenten who is an eighth degree black belt signified by a red belt with a black stripe in the center. A gong is struck three times, and all the students rush into the main training hall arranging themselves by rank with the highest ranking in the front where Shihan Lenten will be. This day Sensei Thomas is dai sempai (highest ranking student), and Shihan will conduct the training.

Shihan enters the training area as Thomas calls out in Japanese, "Kiotsuke, Shihan ni rei" (stand at attention and bow to Shihan). All the students pull right foot to left and bow to Shihan and the pictures of Gichin Funakoshi and the other masters behind him. Sensei Thomas shouts, "*Saiza*," directing the students to assume a squat meditation position with buttocks resting on their heels. This position is used for announcements, meditation, rising blocks, and defense techniques from the ground. A karateka learns to defend him/herself from all positions and angles.

Shihan Lenten speaks. "Today we have a unique situation to discuss, a matter that must be settled as quickly as possible. As many of you know, three attacks by a Chinese consortium have been made on Nidansha Alex. Knowing him like I do over the past many years, I am certain that these attacks were not provoked by him. Alex is a fine example of what we teach here—strength with humility. Karate is a defensive art. Some investigative work by me and Sensei Thomas ties these attempts on his life to a group based in Chinatown below the Sang Su restaurant. We will go there later today and convince them that they must cease and desist these attacks on Alex. Any further attacks on him shall be considered as an attack on all brothers in our kyokai. If we are not diplomatically successful, we will have no choice other than to destroy this consortium which appears to be linked to the CCP leader himself, Dung Zhou Ping."

As Shihan pauses for effect, a Molotov cocktail crashes through the front window in the foyer. Shihan, having been involved in real combat situations, knows exactly what to do. He orders everyone to hit the floor and cover their heads. The ensuing explosion takes out the foyer and wall between them and the entrance. A few students are hit with flying glass, but miraculously, no one is seriously injured—at least they aren't showing it. Never let your opponent know that you're hurt; it can cost you your life in a real confrontation. Once, as an example, Yudansha Greater caught a right cross punch solidly on the left side of his chin. This was done by an enraged green belt. Greater absorbed the punch without even flinching and continued to fight as if nothing happened. He won the fight by TKO soon after the uncontrolled punch hit him leaving his opponent face down on the ground. This is "fighting spirit" that Kanto kata teaches.

Minutes after the explosion, the brothers were joined by the Hawthorne police extinguishing the fire ensuing gasoline explosion. These cops know Sensei Thomas well since he trains or has trained many of them in the martial arts.

Yudansha Dennis, who is late getting to class, sees the perpetrator's car and is pursuing them on his KZ-900, a big four-cylinder Kawasaki motorcycle. After about an hour or so, Dennis calls the dojo and tells Thomas that he has followed them into NYC Chinatown. He observed them going downstairs below Sang Su's restaurant.

Shihan Lenten is livid. Thomas, Lenten, Greater, Ho, Alex, Doc, and the Van deGraff brothers decide enough is enough. They are going to deal with these assassins now. Two cars and two motorcycles leave Hawthorne for NYC Chinatown. The war has begun.

26

LITTLE WAR IN BIG CHINATOWN

Arriving in SoHo around noon, the brothers park their vehicles throughout the Chinatown area. They meet at the junction of Canal and Mulberry Streets to discuss strategy. Ho leaves to walk to the Sang Su restaurant followed by one brother at a time spaced about twenty yards apart. He goes directly downstairs below Sang Su's and sees two well-built Chinese guards. They are standing at an entrance door which bears a sign "Sang Su Computer Systems—Authorized Personnel Only." He thinks, *Why do they need two strong arms at a computer company?* Ho tells them that he is here to talk with Mr. Chu.

"Mr. Chu no work here. No Mr. Chu. You leave now," one of the guards says. Ho insists that Mr. Chu asked him to meet him here at noon for a tour of the computer facility and lunch upstairs after the tour. One of the guards grabs Ho's arm—big mistake. Ho politely asks him to release his arm, but the guard tightens his grip on him in an attempt to escort Ho back up the stairs. Ho places the ball of his foot, toes curled up, between the guard's legs sending him down to the cement floor clutching his cojones. He then grabs and twists the arms of the other guard one hundred eighty degrees flipping him in a loop that ends with the guard crashing onto the floor. By this time the first guard has partially recovered, but Greater is with Ho now. Greater dodges a weak punch then redirects the guard's momentum smashing his head into the concrete wall near the entrance door. Guard one is now unconscious after Greater just neutralized him. Guard two, writhing in pain from his badly bruised arms, gets up and charges Ho with an attempted head butt. Ho side-steps the guard and plants an uppercut to the guard's middle chest area breaking several ribs. Guard two is neutralized lying in extreme pain on the ground.

Now Lenten is there too with Alex; Dennis and Doc are posting guard at the top of the staircase. One of the "computer operators," hearing the commotion, opens the coded locked door. Lenten kicks the door completely open, and it is left hanging on one hinge. One of the operators takes out his gun, but Greater is quickly behind him with his Smith & Wesson 9mm in contact with the head of the gun-wielding man. Ron says, "Drop it or I'll scramble your brains." The man drops his gun immediately unwilling to lose a significant portion of his head.

Ho has all the computer operators line up, face to the red and gold tapestry-covered wall. He looks at the computer monitor and sees the face of Ping. Mistaking Ho for one of his men, Ping asks him in Mandarin whether Alex has been eliminated. Ho says, "Yes, we got him last night. He's dead." Ming hopes this will buy Alex some time to get unwound from the homicidal web that they got him trapped in.

Ping asks Ho about the other China dolls stationed in Manhattan. "Have they successfully infected their American targets with syphilis?"

Ho answers, "Yes, all infected, deaths imminent."

Ping is happy with the report and logs off.

Meanwhile the "computer operator" closest to the back door has signaled for help by tapping a kind of Chinese Morse code on the door. The back door blasts open, and four very able-looking six-foot-plus men charge in and at first confront Shihan Lenten. He was isolated in a section of the basement. They surround him and attack with shuriken, swords, and sai. Within seconds there are weapons being dropped and men's bodies flying in all directions. Messing with an ex-Marine with an eighth degree black belt turns out to be hazardous to their health. Never did anyone see such a big guy move so precisely with speed and agility to incapacitate four robust male attackers. After the four men are neutralized, the basement floor is littered with Ping's soldiers. Lenten and his kyokai members are standing in the center of the room in the midst of unconscious wushu members. The computer people against the walls fear for their lives but without cause. Armed with the information that Ho got from misdirected Ping and the frightened computer operators, the kyokai members take all the hard drives and CDs then destroy the computer center and make their exit. It is now obvious that they must cut off the head of the dragon at the source (Beijing). That is the only way that Alex and the kyokai will be out of future danger. The discs and hard drives will be perused to learn about the source and operational strategy of this conspiracy in the PRC and ROC. Ho was born in the Kowloon Bay area just across from Hong Kong right after WWII. Having him on the team will be a great asset in the next daring phase of the kyokai, viz, retiring the mainland Chinese controlling masterminds and leaders of this foul conspiracy.

Shihan Lenten calls for another strategy meeting, this time in a conference room within the privacy of the Hawthorne police department next to the dojo. Sensei Thomas has access to this room since he has trained many local cops there, and the department reciprocates the favor. The brothers retreat out of Chinatown with a shallow victory to go back to Hawthorne to outline a strategy for a complete victory.

27

HPD STRATEGIC SESSION FOR COMPLETE SUCCESS: CODE NAME "DRAGON SLAYER"

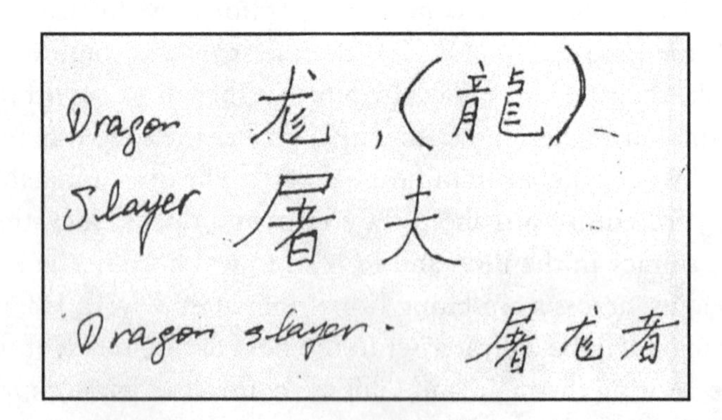

Not being able to return to the fire-damaged dojo, the brothers meet the next day at the conference room in the HPD. This room is furnished with all the modern audio video equipment any speaker could ask for. Today none of it will be necessary, no notes will be taken, and no records will be kept.

Sensei Thomas and Shihan Lenten and associates are planning a covert mission to Beijing after reviewing the hard drives and CDs seized in Chinatown. The China Doll Conspiracy has been analyzed with regard to what, where, when, why, and how and is now out in the open. The dragon's head must be removed at the residence of the dragon. Failure is not an option since the USA itself is at risk of total domination by Ping's CCP. The American intelligence sources have failed to perceive this threat and are tangled in a bureaucratic conundrum with their hands shackled as if handcuffed.

Initial plans are for Thomas and Ho to enter Beijing using fictitious passports with false identities and find the location of Ping's transmissions and office. Ping will be observed to document his itinerary and usual routes of activity. His points of vulnerability are to be gleaned and schedule of activities documented. This information will be transmitted to Hong Kong where Alex and Dennis will be waiting. There is the hope that the China doll's training center can be breached and ultimately destroyed. Lenten will be in Taipei with a small force of dans and in direct contact with both Alex and Thomas via wireless, secure internet connections to their palm tops. Lenten has learned that Tianjin, near Beijing, is where the bulk of the Chinese army is stationed at the beck and call of Ping; therefore, Tianjin is to be avoided.

Greater and Doc are going to Nepal arriving in Kathmandu about the same time that Ho and Thomas get to Beijing. They are to covertly enter Tibet, locate the monastery prison, and destroy the Chinese occupying force and liberate the China doll's relatives held captive there. They will be disguised as Tibetan monks and claim that they are on a pilgrimage to the Shen Shu Zong temple in the Himalayas to praise Buddha; they're just stopping for a rest at the occupied Zen Tao temple in the mountains.

Upon receipt of Lenten's information, Alex and Dennis will locate the Hong Kong/Kowloon training facility; wait for backup; then neutralize the instructors, trainers, and guards. The China dolls will be liberated, free to return to their homes. This training facility will be totally destroyed using several cases of C-4 that Ho arranged to have delivered to them.

The meeting at the HPD adjourned at 1530. There is no written or taped record of this meeting. There was no meeting as far as any evidence could tell. Each kyokai brother knows what he must do. A handful of extremely disciplined and capable black belts is essentially taking on the entire Chinese army of Ping. The key to success is to keep Ping in the dark. Total secrecy so he doesn't suspect a thing.

Summary of Operations for Mission **"Dragon Slayer"**

1.) Lenten is communications central and is stationed in Taipei, Taiwan. He supplies and relays information found in Ping's hard drives and the archives of China.
2.) Doc and Greater are to go to Kathmandu, Nepal, to prepare for the journey to Tibet. Disguised as Buddhist monks, they will proceed to Lhasa, Tibet, to pilgrimage to the mountain temple to free the China doll's relatives being held hostage and retire any resistance as necessary.
3.) Ho and Thomas are to go to Beijing where Ping has his worldwide operational headquarters and destroy it with extreme prejudice.
4.) Alex and Dennis will wait in Hong Kong/Kowloon Bay area for the other four men upon completion of their missions. The six men will take out the China doll training center with explosives and free the dolls.
5.) All six men will then proceed to the Hong Kong airport and book first class passage to Taipei, Taiwan, to meet with Lenten and his associates.
6.) After a complete review of operations by Lenten, the entire kyokai brotherhood will return to the USA.

28

DOC AND GREATER GO TO NEPAL

At roughly the same time that Ho and Thomas arrive in Beijing, Doc and Greater are touching down in Kathmandu, Nepal. It's about two hours earlier here than in Beijing. Their hotel, the Regency, is a short walk past prayer wheels and butter lamps on ledges everywhere. Monkeys are all over the streets and quite aggressive if they perceive food being consumed by a human.

After checking in, Doc heads to a specific souvenir store that Lenten sourced as a place where Buddhist monk clothing could be purchased with no questions asked, just cash. The clerk descends into the basement joined by Doc stepping down on a rat-infested dirt floor. As soon as the lights are turned on, the rats scurry in all directions. There is a teak wood cabinet against the red/orange-draped wall with several locks on it. The clerk opens it with old-fashioned double-teethed keys, and a stack of orange gowns are neatly stacked therein. Doc picks out two that would loosely fit him and Greater. He hands a crisp American fifty-dollar bill to the clerk, and both return upstairs to the souvenir shop. The clerk puts the uniforms in a plain unlabeled brown paper bag. Doc thanks the clerk and walks back to the hotel. On the way to the hotel elevator, there is a soda machine. The price of a 330 mL Coca-Cola is one American quarter; this is a lot cheaper than the one to two dollars that vendors in NYC charge. In this country, everything is for sale, including the rented room, and is inexpensive if you have US money from your overpaid job in the States. Fifteen dollars/ day for the hotel room is unheard of since the 1950s in America.

The next day Doc and Greater get their hair shaved off to mimic the Buddhist monks. However, not much can be done about their round eyes and Caucasian noses. Fortunately, the brothers both have small noses that are somewhat flat. Their eyes are also slightly almond from squinting in the sun during early morning workouts.

Upon returning to their hotel room, they try on their orange gowns. A loose fit is standard for the monks. Next on their list is to arrange transportation to the Nepal–Tibet border. Helicopters are available but too costly for an inconspicuous pair on monks, so they choose to book a train or bus. Anyone renting a helicopter, especially a pair of monks with little funds, would look very, very unusual. There is no direct bus route from Kathmandu to Lhasa, Tibet, except for a tour bus. The two monks purchase tickets and Tibet travel visas for this long bus trip. The road is never in good condition, and the ride is long and taxing, especially when it reaches sixteen thousand feet above sea level. Lhasa is Tibet's most populated city and lies at about three thousand six hundred meters or eleven thousand eight hundred feet elevation. Although small compared with NYC (the Big Apple), this little apricot already has prostitution, street drugs, pollution, and trucks backed up on congested main streets. Fortunately, the brothers won't be staying long there as their pilgrimage is to the Zen Toa Mountain Monastery outside of Lhasa. This is where the China doll's relatives are being kept under Chinese guards. It's a one-day journey by 4WD vehicle to get to its parking lot (a noted high mountain tourist attraction). Once there, there is a steep climb up wooden stairs to the mountain view monastery entrance. This doesn't present a problem for the two American monks since both are in top physical condition from their martial arts workouts. However, Doc became a little short of breath when the bus rides over the sixteen-thousand-foot ridge en route to Zen Toa. He is functioning much better at twelve thousand feet. The monastery is controlled by the Chinese army who allows monks to come into pray for a few hours each day. It's Doc and Greater's good fortune to be here on a Saturday since most of the guards have gone to Lhasa to indulge in drugs, alcohol, and prostitution.

At the entrance to the monastery, one Chinese soldier checks and validates the Tibetan visas of the American monks. The monks now climb the steep staircase to access the main prayer room. Inside are two guards, and little Tao is sweeping the floor. One guard stops Doc at the entrance to check his credentials and then slaps his face in a show of disrespect to Buddhism. While the other guard goes out to the high perched balcony, Doc grabs his guard, spins him around, and snaps his neck. The guard drops to the floor like a lead balloon, quite dead from a broken wind pipe. The other guard, upon hearing the commotion, comes running into the main room with his rifle ready to fire. He meets Greater's thrusting ball of his foot launching him into the purple velvet tapestry mounted on the wall. Dazed by the force of the kick, he slowly gets up sans his rifle. Greater gives him a straight jab with his locked fingers to his Adam's apple. The guard starts gasping for air then drops like a rock. Upon checking for his pulse, Doc pronounces him no longer among the living.

Little Tao, seeing the two guards dispatched, runs to Greater and gives him a hug. He then leads them to the chambers below where the hostages are imprisoned. Tao knows where the keys to the cells are kept and shows Doc. They open all the cages, and Tao tells them in Mandarin that they are free. The group remains in the main room while Greater descends the monastery staircase. He is met by the first guard who is pointing a rifle at him. Greater hits the rifle barrel with his rising left forearm, grabs the butt spinning the rifle around into his possession. The guard is now looking down the barrel of his own rifle. A load crack is heard as the rifle butt hits the face of the guard who is now bleeding from a broken nose. Another blow across the right shoulder causes the guard to drop prostrate on the ground. With the final strike of the rifle butt to the guard's head, Greater watches his head come apart in pieces.

Signaling to Doc, the hostages are led down the stairs and into the parking lot where several vehicles are parked. Some of the vehicles have the keys still in the ignition, others Greater hot-wires to start them. Doc, through bilingual Tao, asks and gets volunteers to drive each vehicle. The rest of the hostages fill the available vehicles. Greater convinces the tourist bus driver to drive the filled bus with the remaining hostages back to Lhasa. The other vehicles will follow him back to the city. From Lhasa, the hostages can recruit Han Chinese Tibetans to drive them to Kathmandu and freedom. After that, they are on their own. To facilitate the cooperation of the Han, Greater gives each hostage enough yuan for the drivers who will be instructed to use back unguarded roads to get to Nepal. Doc, Greater, and the tour bus driver take the bus back to Kathmandu the way they came since all have visas. Upon arriving in Nepal, the brothers shed the orange monk garments in their room. They eat supper at the hotel restaurant then pack their bags and check out.

A short walk among the monkeys, butter lamps, and prayer wheels brings them to the Nepal International Airport. Using a secure internet connection, mission accomplished is sent to Ho in Beijing and Alex in Kowloon Bay. Two hours later the plane departs for Hong Kong. Here, if necessary, they will assist as needed destroying the China doll training center. The trainee women will be released with the knowledge that their relatives have been safely evacuated from the prison at Zen Toa Mountain Monastery. The hostages will have to decide if they wish to return to their Chinese homes and risk being recaptured, staying in Nepal, or getting transportation to a neighboring country like Bhutan or upper Mongolia.

29

THOMAS AND HO'S JOURNEY TO BEIJING

Ho and Thomas board the 747 for Beijing International Airport on a nonstop eighteen-hour flight from EWR (Newark, NJ). The plane is only about half full leaving center rows of five seats for weary travelers to sleep on. However, it's impossible to get any rest during the flight since people are constantly moving about. Unintelligible chatter of several languages fills the volume of the coach passenger section. Many Chinese nationals are on board returning to their homeland. Some have concluded lucrative business deals, while others are students from educational stays at Ivy League universities. Most of them are not accompanied by wives or children since their relatives weren't permitted to travel to the USA as an insurance against defections. This is a policy taken out by Ping's government to ensure that his Ivy League PhDs come back to fortify the science curricula in China. The cold war left China woefully poor academically in talent, facilities, and labs.

Ho blends right in being an ROC nationalist from the Hong Kong area prior to 1999. Thomas sticks out like a sore thumb due to his big Caucasian nose and lack of almond eyes. His Fu Manchu mustache/beard combination is the right beard on the wrong round-eyed face.

As the plane ascends, a strong typically Newark airport cross-wind causes extreme turbulence which causes many Chinese passengers to reach for their barf bags. They are unaccustomed to air travel due to poor salaries and heavy restrictions given them by their government. Ho finds this humorous, laughing loudly and nudging Thomas to "check this out."

As the plane settles down, one of the PRC nationals unfastens his seatbelt and walks over to Ho who is still strapped in as advised during the turbulence. He looks at Ho and says in Mandarin, "You are a traitor. You travel with this American pig. You must be punished for this and for laughing at your countrymen."

Ho looks up at the offending Chinaman, raises his arms, and, as the sleeves of his shirt fall, exposes a dragon on one forearm and a tiger on the other burned into his flesh. The offending Chinaman immediately apologizes and begs that Ho will forgive him. Before Ho says anything, the man quickly rushes back to his seat. You can hear much whispering in Mandarin as the offender tells others about the burnt-in dragon and tiger. These animal symbols are the marks of a Shaolin priest, symbols of kung fu expertise seen only on the senior monks of the White Crane system of kung fu.

Thomas asks, "What's going on, Ho? Who was that guy, and what did he say?"

Ho cracks a small smile and says, "He called me a traitor because I'm traveling with an American pig. However, he changed his mind and apologized."

Thomas pursues this incident. "He called me a pig? That's funny because I thought that he looked more like a pig with those flared nostrils of his. Maybe I should go back there and talk with him about this."

Ho grabs Thomas's arm to settle him down and says, "Let it go. We'll pick our fights, not get provoked into them. The guy's a big-mouth jerk unworthy of you exerting yourself to change his attitude." Thomas agrees with Ho and sits back down. What is it with the PRC men? Are they all rude and negative about Americans?

The big Cathay airlines plane lands smoothly on the tarmac at landing strip #6 and taxies to the CA terminal. As people get their hand-carry luggage together, all the Chinese behind Thomas and Ho remain seated and silent. Ho unfastens his seat belt and glances backward to observe all of them rise and bow to him. He returns the gesture with a smirk on his face. It seems that respect for a Shaolin has carried over to the new China.

The two brothers deplane and retrieve their luggage which stands in a primitive pile outside the plane since this terminal has no automated luggage delivery system. Outside the airport doors, Ho signals for a cab. A pre-arranged driver picks them up in his small standard shift 160E Mercedes. The driver, whose name is Wen Chu, a secret member of the Falun Gong association banned by the PRC, loads their suitcases in the trunk and opens the rear door of the medium brown Benz. As they sit down in the vehicle, Chu speaks in Hunan Chinese. "Sifu, how long will you be staying in China?"

Ho answers, "We're not sure. Our visas are good for thirty days. It depends on many things concerning our business here."

Chu responds, "Depends on what factors?"

Ho responds, "It depends on what cooperation we receive with our business here."

With that said, the cab pulls away from the curb as Chu passes a package over the front seat to Ho—two untraceable Glock G19 9mm pistols. Upon further opening of the package, there are four extra magazines with seventeen rounds each and two custom-made silencers as well as other tools. Ho is well connected with Falun Gong associates throughout the mainland and in the new territories where he is from.

Thomas stuffs the Glock behind his belt at the small of his back. Ho puts his in his sport coat vest side pocket leading to a noticeable bulge over his heart.

The taxi stops at the Peking House where the two Americans check in using their fictitious passports as identification. Although prostitution is illegal in the PRC, a few scantily clad young women are wandering around the reception area. They smile sweetly at Ho and Thomas as they follow the busboy pushing a cart with their luggage to the elevator. No time for pleasure, especially entrapment pleasure, at this moment. Many of the girls work with the Chinese government. They try to seduce foreigners so that they go to their rooms with them. Within ten minutes, the police arrive and arrest the foreigner. He now has to pay one thousand dollars for his release and another one thousand dollars for the girl too.

Upon arriving on the sixteenth floor, the brothers scrutinize the hallway looking for the emergency exits in case they need to make a hasty retreat. The busboy gives them a dirty look as they fail to tip him. Unlike Japan where no one tips for standard services, everyone in China has their hand out. Their luggage rests in front of rooms 1613 and 1614, two rooms joined by an inner door chosen for security of each brother. This will be their home while they are on their "sales" mission. Ho looks out the sixteenth-floor window and sees the effect of a capitalist economy that took over China when Ping opened the country to foreigners. The streets below are packed with many well-known Western fast-food restaurants. There is McDonald's, Burger King, Sbarro, Colonel Sanders, and Starbucks among the designer clothing stores. This area looks like a shopping mall in Paramus, NJ.

Spring boom cranes are scattered around the city, and new construction of high risers is robust. Among the new buildings are signs of the old pre-boom China. On the back streets, small shops are coupled together like row housing, some with just one light bulb dangling in the wind. This is where the little guy does business, but the sight of this ghetto-like area tends to be avoided by visitors. However, this is also where you can negotiate a cheap price for, e.g., a silk tie or tea set. Many have small refrigerators holding cold drinks for the wandering tourists. One dollar can buy quite a bit since it is equal to 8.7 yuan. Most vendors will take dollars in place of yuan, a convenient way to overcharge for commodities. After you finish your drink, there are several people wrestling for your empty bottle. Another sign of capitalism that was adopted was money for returned empty bottles.

The paved streets below are nearly gridlocked with cars alongside mule-driven carts, bicycles, pedestrians, and taxi cabs. This is to be expected since Beijing is the capital city and closest to the Great Wall. The USA astronauts remarked that you could see the Great Wall from outer space, weather permitting.

Gugong, aka the Forbidden City, is near here and is a popular tourist attraction being much more valuable open than it was forbidden. In Gugong, the Imperial Palace is located, and this is where Ping is likely to have his base of operations. Ping outraged the world when he ordered his army to clear nearby Tiananmen Square of protesters where a large billboard of Mao oversees the area; many students were murdered.

Thomas snaps Ho back to contemporary reality. "Ming, Ming! Let's get something to eat." Ming is thinking dim sum while Thomas is thinking a medium rare ribeye.

Early the next morning (06:00), Ho is practicing soft kung fu which he refers to as tai chi chuan. This soft form is very popular in the PRC, and you will find people throughout China practicing it in parks throughout the city. Thomas gets up and heads for a cold shower, saying, "Ooohhwa," as the iced water hits his skin. His weary muscles are being rudely awakened. Ho, watering the carpet with his sweat, follows him as soon as Thomas is toweling. Both boys dressed in drab, loose clothing and head down to the cafeteria. This hotel offers a full Western breakfast of scrambled eggs or omelets, bacon, orange juice, tea or coffee, plus a plethora of less Western items. After the meal, they leave the hotel and head for the hotel shuttle that goes to the Imperial Palace. They are carrying concealed Glock 19s and assorted firearms accessories which hide well in their baggy pants and shirts left untucked.

When they get to the palace, the elite palace guards in drab green military suits are marching in formation goose stepping in cadence to a drum beat. Ping observes them from a third-story balcony attired in full military uniform laden with all sorts of colored medals pinned to it. When the drill is completed, Ping disappears into the third-floor vestibule. Ho turns to Thomas, saying, "This building is a red and gold fortress. It will be very difficult to enter through any exterior door or gate." Two soldiers are posted at each direction, N-S-E-W.

They return to the hotel and wirelessly contact Lenten in Taipei, Taiwan. He has been perusing the palace and Great Wall architecture and has found a secret tunnel in the literature blueprints of the area. The tunnel leads from the Great Wall to a chamber underneath the Imperial Palace, an escape route designed during the Ming dynasty. Lenten sends the coordinates of the Great Wall portal along with an old map to Ho. Tomorrow Ho and Thomas will purchase tourist tickets for the Great Wall and locate the portal.

It's early morning again in Beijing, and the brothers conclude their a.m. routines and head to the concierge. They purchase tickets for the Great Wall tour and get on the hotel transport jitney. At the entrance, Ho hands the attendant the kanji-printed entry tickets.

Lenten has cautioned them to look for ground-level gates on the China side of the wall. This is where the soldiers enter and use a ladder inside the wall to reach the flat surface on the top of the wall. All the gates are guarded by at least four CCP soldiers. Walking further on the wall, they reach one of several strategically located beacon towers. These are small partially enclosed rooms that served to deliver messages to other beacon towers by flame and smoke signals. This primitive alert system signaled the arrival of enemy brigades along the thirteen-thousand-plus-mile-long wall. Upon reaching the sixth beacon tower from the entrance, Thomas notes that visitors have been using it as a latrine since it reeks of urine. It reminds him of the NYC subway system. There are no guards at this sixth tower that Lenten sent them to examine since the archives mention access to the palace from here. Thomas peruses the structure and finds a very well-hidden latch on the floor. Tempted to pull it up, Ho whistles to him signaling that a sentry is walking toward them. The sentry is about ten feet from them. Thomas kicks some red brick shavings over the latch to cover it.

The sentry peeks into the beacon tower then resumes walking up the wall. Lenten's research implied that under the latch is a man-sized hole cover. When lifted, it leads to a tunnel that ends in a hidden inner chamber in the Imperial Palace. According to legend, Emperor Ming had slaves carve out this tunnel as an escape route for the emperor should Beijing be overrun by one of China's many enemies. This is the route that Thomas and Ho will take to get into the palace undetected; the tunnel hasn't been used in the last two centuries, and the Chinese have essentially forgotten about it.

Thomas and Ho walk back to the entrance and bus back to the hotel. Every evening at dusk the tourist entrance is closed for the day.

After dinner and preparations, at exactly 2:00 a.m., the brothers fully equip themselves with some tools, rope, Glocks, and silencers and put on light sneakers. They reach the wall by electric scooter "borrowed" from in front of the hotel. They enter the turf on the China side of the wall at an isolated location where they cut through a six-foot fence. There is a three-meter ladder which takes them to the top surface of the wall. They stealthily walk to the beacon tower which has the floor latch and, presumably, manhole cover. No guards appear to be posted anywhere near this section of the wall. Upon arriving at the designated beacon tower, Ho brushes off the dirt covering the latch, and both men get their crowbars ready in anticipation of lifting the heavy manhole cover. Thomas pries the cover up about 3 cm as Ho uses his bar to further raise this cast iron, heavily rusted manhole cover. Leaving the crowbars in place, both use their gloved hands to raise it completely off the underlying manhole. Shining an LED flashlight into the hole, Ho sees a dirt floor about three meters below. There is an old wooden ladder leaning at the top of this entrance. Ho, being only around 65 kg and much lighter than Thomas, starts to descend into the dark, musty chamber below. Few Chinese people knew that there was a hollowed-out pathway in the center of wall leading to other areas of the wall. Faint beams of light from nearby modern buildings push through the crevasses in the side cement wall. Black bats are abundant near these cracks and on most of the ceiling.

Before Thomas joins Ho, he fastens a thick rope to a pillar of the beacon tower in case the ladder fails under his weight. As he descends, one of the rungs of the ladder snaps, dropping him quickly to the next lower rung. That rung holds, and Thomas completes his descent. Stale, musty odors emit from this area, and human bones are scattered on the dirt floor. There are also swords, shields, arrows, bows, and assorted ancient Chinese weapons of war unrecognizable to them lying in the dirt. Many arachnids lay still as they detect motion. Some are as large as a golf ball clinging to ledges on the inner walls.

Thomas and Ho proceed slowly in the direction of the Imperial Palace weary of booby traps that may be present. There are fluorescent kanji characters and arrows pointing in the direction of the palace. Ho is able to read the characters and leads Thomas as he follows the signs. Something lurches at Ho who falls back shining the light on the surprise. Thomas chuckles. "Don't let that frog beat you up." Ho doesn't laugh and points to the spiders on Thomas's jacket. Thomas freaks out immediately shedding his coat while Ho dusts off the remaining spiders.

Further down the path there is a muddy section underpart of the wall that's been cracked for centuries. They slosh through the mud burying their sneakers in it. In the distance there appears to be a jaded door of sorts. It has an ancient well-rusted lock securing it. Thomas uses his crowbar quickly dispatching it. Iron doesn't weather well in damp, musty cave-like conditions. It has become brittle iron(III) oxide (ferric oxide) which crumbles when any force is applied to it.

Ho reads the embossed kanji characters then tells Thomas that the palace is about one thousand meters ahead. Two hundred meters further toward the palace they encounter a ditched of unknown depth filled with filthy, muddy, putrid-smelling water. Thomas takes a sword of about 1.5 meters and inserts it into the ditch. The water appears to be about one meter deep. Fortunately, there is a crudely shaped, roughly three inches by ten inches board about three meters long leaning on the wall on their side of the ditch. With the board positioned over the ditch, Ho is first to try its strength. It holds. Thomas, at 90 kgs, starts the trip as the board sags but holds. The board is left in place in case a return trip is necessary.

Advancing another two hundred yards, they encounter barbed wire from floor to ceiling. After testing it for electric shock potential and finding none, they take out their wire cutters that were used on the outside fence. In a few minutes with both men clipping, a wide oval hole is available as an entrance through the barbed wire. Another one hundred yards toward their goal they encounter multiple dog-sized rats. Thomas makes a torch from some red paper on the floor wrapped around a wooden stick. He lights it and uses it to drive the rats further down the tunnel through the barbed wire away from their forward direction.

In front of them is a faded red- and gold-gilded door. It is tightly sealed not budging when it is body-slammed by Thomas. It is unclear what is holding it in place. Upon dusting off centuries of mud and dirt, three hinges are evident. There are also iron spikes about the size of 20D common nails on the perimeter of the door, apparently meant to seal it permanently. The crowbars come out, and the rusted hinges snap like dry pieces of wood. Working the iron spikes along the perimeter of this 1.8-meter-high door (average height of a Chinese man is about 167 cm), the nails start to break due to their age and heavily rusted conditions. With the door freed from its stays, Ho slowly opens it and steps through. He encounters a series of bear paw-like traps, probably from the nineteenth century. Thomas follows his path around the traps to avoid losing a leg. About twenty meters further, they enter a large room with seventeenth- and eighteenth-century torture devices hanging on the walls. At the far end of the room is a wooden staircase leading up to a gray metal door with a freezer-type lock handle. They can hear the faint sound of voices on the other side of the door. Both men cock their Glocks and screw on the custom-made silencers. Strangely, the lock on the door is open, so no need for the crowbars. While Ho very slowly opens the door, Thomas has his Glock positioned to fire. One of the guards behind the door has his Russian AK-47 barrel protruding through the slight opening. With Ho behind the door and Thomas crouched on the right side at the bottom of the staircase, the guard doesn't see either man when he enters the room. *Pfstttt, pfsttt,* and the silent bullets leave Thomas's gun and enter the chest of the guard. The guard drops down the staircase ending up prone face down on the floor. A second guard runs into the room, and Ho pulls his rifle through as he pumps three 9mm bullets into his chest. He falls on top of the first guard at the base of the stairs. As the Americans wait silently behind the door, they hear nothing. Ho slowly opens the door peering in and sees some tables and chairs. There is smoke rising from an unfinished cigarette in an ashtray on one of the tables. There are also two partially filled glasses and a pack of Lucky Strike cigarettes on the other table. A pair of dice and some yuan notes in troughs on the second table gives the appearance of some gambling occurring here. No other guards are present in the room.

The room has two additional doors. One is marked exit, and the other one has a Chinese placard saying, "main war room." Suddenly the exit door opens, and two well-endowed Western women scantily clothed come into the room. Both are dressed with colorful Chinese lingerie and appear ready for action. Ho points his Glock at them and tells them in Mandarin and English to be quiet if they don't wish to get hurt. Thomas looks at Ho and says, "What the hell do we do now?" Ho gags both with cloth from the recently deceased guards. He then applies pressure to a pressure point on each girl's neck. Thomas catches one woman as she falls asleep, and Ho holds the other. The two unconscious women are placed in the chairs in a slumped-over position as if sleeping. Thomas asks Ho what he did, and Ho explains that he used a Shaolin technique to put them into a deep sleep. "You definitely have to teach me that when we get home," says Thomas. Ho assures Thomas that the technique is as effective as Rohypnol in inducing unconsciousness for many hours.

Looking through a peephole in the main war room door, Thomas sees what appears to be four bikini-clad women working on keyboards with monitors all hooked up to mainframe computers. This is likely where Ping's orders go out and field reports come in. There is also a wireless H/P printer in the room.

The Americans pause to review their mission here. Destroy all hard drives in the mainframe computers, secure the women, and deal with Ping—whereabouts unknown at the moment. Escape back to the hotel area from the Imperial Palace.

Ho and Thomas enter the main war room with Glocks ready. The four Asian women are startled and told to be silent. Ho tells them to stand against the back wall then gags three of the four with cloth. The fourth is directed to call Ping to the war room. She pees in her bikini from fright but does what she is told. Then she joins the other three sound asleep.

After a few minutes pass, Ping enters the room via the front wall door. He is being escorted by two guards. Thomas quickly dispatches the guards with his silent Glock leaving Ping standing alone. Ho tells him in Mandarin to stay quiet or face the fate of his two guards. Thomas motions to Ping for him to lie prone on the ground face down. Although Ho renders the four women unconscious the Shaolin way, he has a different plan for Ping. He retrieves a small brown leather pouch from an inner pocket which contains a mixture of herbs. He takes one of the water bottles near one keyboard and mixes the powder into it. With a gun in contact with Ping's left temple, he orders Ping to sit up and drink this mixture. Fearing for his life, Ping quickly complies. Ping lapses into unconsciousness within two minutes. His heart is barely beating, giving the appearance that he is dead. However, Ping is not dead, just paralyzed. He was given a secret herbal mix that only high-standing Shaolin priests have access to. Ho secured these special herbs from a Chinatown pharmacy in Manhattan where the chemist refused to comply until he was shown the branded-in tiger and dragon on Ho's forearms. Seeing these signs, the chemist bowed low and prepared the mixture without further delay. It slows and quiets the heartbeat and totally relaxes the body giving the appearance of death to the taker.

With all resistance subdued, Thomas and Ho destroy the mainframes, shatter the hard drives, and take the zip drives with them. To ensure complete destruction of this computer network, Thomas riddles the computer accessories with 9mm bullets causing plastic electronic pieces to fly in all directions. Ho then points to the door that they came in indicating that it's time to leave.

The two dans go out the same way they entered. Ho leads the way out the war room door toward the Great Wall tunnel passing dead guards already in rigor. Back into the tunnel part of the wall they notice light streaming through some cracks in the wall. Since it is getting dark outside, Thomas suggests breaking through this weak area where the light is coming from. He offers this to Ho as an alternative to retracing their steps through the multiple hazards going back to the beacon tower. Ho couldn't agree more, and the two men start hacking at the crack with their crowbars. Using these tools and some logs lying on the floor, they made a two-thirds meter roughly circular hole to the outside world. Peering outside, Thomas sees no guards or sentries nearby and goes completely through to the exterior of the Great Wall. Ho follows Thomas on the dirt, mud, and grass tracing a path to the cut perimeter fence. At the fence, the scooter is still there. They shed all excess clothes and tools, restart the scooter, and head back to the hotel.

Once there, they take quick showers and call for a Mercedes taxi to get to the Beijing airport. They didn't bother to check out of the hotel to make it appear that they were just going out for the night life. Upon arriving at the urine-stench airport, Ho purchases two tickets on a United 767 to Hong Kong which is boarding in five minutes. At gate 62 leaving for Hong Kong at 19:00, they pre-board with first-class tickets and pass the stewardess checking credentials with their fictitious passports. So far they're having no problems using fake credentials as they board the half-filled plane. All the airport security detect no implements, e.g., crowbars, Glocks, etc., because they left them scattered around the Great Wall fence.

Two hours later, after a few short typical airliner delays, they arrive in Hong Kong. Greater and Doc, having completed their mission in Tibet, meet them at the luggage carousel. The last part of their mission is to link up with Alex and Dennis. Then the six men will go to the Hong Kong/Kowloon Bay China doll training center and destroy it. Lenten in Taipei has given them the location which he obtained from his friends in the CIA. The four recently joined together men are sitting in the hotel bar area, drinking Shirley Temples and snacking on seaweed-covered pretzels as they await word from Alex and Dennis. They have booked two rooms in the Hong Kong Gardens, which they may not be using depending on the success of the mission. Now they just sit and wait.

30

THE AMERICANS DESTROY THE TRAINING CENTER

Contacting a member of the Falun Gong resistance, a courier brings Alex and Dennis hand grenades, guns, C-4 with caps, remote igniters, and flares all made in America. They leave these tools in an empty oil barrel on a friendly Chinese junk boat moored in the harbor. Many Falun Gong members own these junks which were registered before this area was returned to the PRC.

At 17:00, Alex and Dennis met up with the other four Americans at the hotel. The group of men proceed to the waterfront area where Lenten informed them of the location of the training facility. There are students' protests against the CCP which are preoccupying the harbor police. The six men make their way through the crowds and arrive at pier 16. There is a large vacant red brick building that Lenten informed them containing the training center. The China dolls should be two floors below the dock level of this edifice.

As Alex and Dennis retrieve the "tool kit" from the junk, Ho approaches a guard by the building side entrance. In Mandarin, Ho asks the guard to let him pass through the side door. The guard looks at him in disbelief and pushes Ho back away from the door, saying (in Mandarin), "Who the hell are you? Get lost or I'll—" He suddenly stops speaking as Ho smashes the guard's head into the wall with a vicious spinning back kick rendering him bleeding profusely collapsed on the waterfront deck. Ho pulls up on the guard's shirt and punches him in the mouth sending him to a state of unconsciousness.

After witnessing this brutal attack, the five other men rush toward the side door of this apparently vacant building. Alex fires a silenced .45 caliber bullet at the lock, and it unlocks cleanly. He says to Ho, "I thought the warrior code of Bushido teaches us to use minimum force to subdue the opponent."

Ho replies, "I guess I forgot the code when he put his hands on me and pushed. I'll behave myself from now on." Alex smiles at Ho's awesomeness. The others now join Ho and Alex inside the vacant harbor level room.

At the south side in the room, there is a hallway. It leads them to a service elevator closed in cage like. Alex pushes a call button to summon the lift to the harbor floor level. Dennis opens the cage gate and steps in with Alex following. Both secure their firearms assuring the silencers are fixed tightly. This seems like the logical thing to do since they don't know what to expect two levels down. Dennis pushes the B2 button assuming it will take them to basement level 2.

When the elevator reaches B2, the first look through the cage fence doesn't show any sign of humans moving about. Not enamored by the lack of people, Alex returns the elevator to the harbor level. After his report to the others waiting in the deck level vacant room, the group decides to look for another way to reach the second lower level per Lenten's instructions. Far off on the east side is another somewhat narrow hallway leading to a Dutch door. Ho reads the Chinese symbols on the door aloud to the others, "Training Center BB2 this way." He goes through the bottom half of the door slowly, crouching down with his firearm at ready. He sees a staircase with arrows pointing down to the training center. All of the men quietly descend the staircase until they hear voices. Four of the men remain still on the third step from the landing while Ho and Alex descend to the landing. There, crouching low, they peek through a large window and see several China dolls dressed in just nipple-exposed bras and panties. It's cold and damp down here, and some of the dolls are shivering. There are two soldiers standing at each end of the window with their backs to the windowed wall. The female instructor built like a man is shouting out instructions in Mandarin for the girls to follow. This causes a few of the dolls to pass out (faint) from a combination of fear and exhaustion. The two soldiers abandon their AKs and go to the fainted women. They grab their arms and drag them into another room. Ho thinks positively that this must be some kind of recovery room. The soldiers had left their AK-47s leaning on the wall so that they could remove the unconscious women. It seems like a golden opportunity for the kyokai team to breach the training room.

Alex traces his steps back to the others waiting on the staircase. He leads them to Ho's position near the window but staying out of sight. Armed with firearms and explosives, Ho and Dennis watch the guards return to their stations with their backs to the wall. Ho and Dennis fire their guns through the wall, and the bullets strike the guards. Greater and Doc crash through the tempered glass window and finish the guards off. Another guard in the room points his AK-47 at Greater but feels the sting of two bullets from Alex's muffled 1911 (.45 caliber handgun) then drops to the floor. Thomas leaps into the room and is sparring with the woman instructor who is well trained in wushu. She launches a viscous front kick at him which misses him by millimeters as he deflects it and grabs hold of her leg. Raising the leg above his head causes her to fall backward onto the floor. He gets on top of her and renders her unconscious with a solid punch to her chin.

The dolls in the room are terrified at this bloody scene fearing for their own lives. Ho reassures them that his team is here to free them and no harm will be inflicted on any of them. Ho tells them to follow Thomas and Greater to the stairs to the harbor level. The dolls are shivering as they ascend the stairs to the harbor level. Thomas gently removes the clothes pins and other torture devices from their bodies. They remain in the harbor level empty room in silence under the protection of Thomas and Greater.

Alex signals to Ho to look at the door with the chemical formula and structure of fentanyl on it. There is a faint odor of either acetone or diethyl ether in the training room. These chemicals are used as solvents and in the synthesis of many illicit drugs. Alex is a chemist and can easily recognize these liquids having used them himself as solvents.

The two Americans walk to the fentanyl-labeled door and open it just a crack. They hear laughter and voices from the floors below. Venturing through, they are at another staircase which goes down further into the subbasement areas. Alex proceeds slowly down with Ho following three flights of stairs down to B5B. There is another door with a caution sign on it that reads, "highly flammable." Peeking through a small opening in the door, there seems to be a large room with forty-two-gallon drums stacked in it. Ho reads the characters on the drums then informs Alex that they are filled with acetone, a highly flammable universal solvent. It is such a good solvent that it must be stored in non-plastic containers since it dissolves most plastics and synthetics. It is also very volatile, evaporating almost instantly when exposed to air. There is Chinese music and several people further down this area. They appear to be packaging white powdery chemicals for export to other drug-addicted countries. It is well known that the Chinese have been smuggling fentanyl across the Mexican American border using illegal immigrants as their mules.

It is clear to Alex and Ho what must be done. This is another means to destroy America using drugs instead of toxic women. Alex places C-4 charges with miniature receivers on several of the drums. Ho sets more C-4 on the bottom of the walls in this room. Clumsily, Alex drops one of the metal receivers on the floor, and it makes a distinctive metallic clang as it hits a drum. Activated by the noise, one of the guards from the prep room comes to investigate. Alex is hidden behind some drums, and Ho startles the guard by jumping behind him. He grabs his neck and twists it firmly causing the guard to become limp. Ho then moves the body out of the aisle placing it behind some brown shipping containers.

The C-4 with the acetone vapors will produce a large explosion followed by an uncontrollable fire. The receivers attached to the C-4 will ignite when Alex keys in a secret combination of numbers on his cell phone. Once the sequence is entered and send initiated, all the C-4 packs will be ignited and explode. The remaining C-4 charges are brought up and attached to the walls of the training floor and in the staircases. With the building set to be demolished, the two Americans move up to the room at the level of the harbor.

Greater, Thomas, Dennis, and Doc lead the dolls to a Falun Gong-owned junk in the harbor. They board the junk which will take them across the bay to a secure Falun Gong location away from the activity of the city of Hong Kong. The dolls and men will be supplied with civilian clothes and fake passports. The men will get British passports, and the women will receive Malaysian passports. There are blue and white buses waiting to transport them to ships to take them to Taipei. The four men will escort them to Taipei, Taiwan, to join Lenten and his assistants.

Alex and Ho will return through the rioters and trigger the C-4 explosives while in the midst of this noisy scenario. They'll then return to their hotel, change, and go to the Hong Kong airport for departure to Taiwan. All their tools still with them will be abandoned in the hotel's heating vents.

31

THE RESULTS AND THE DISPOSITION OF THE TEAM

The massive explosion within the vacant harbor level building added substantially to the already chaotic scene in Hong Kong. Half of the building was demolished with bricks, wood, and cement raining down on the police and rioters close to it. Several rioters and police were knocked unconscious by flying debris. The intense flames that followed the blast caused severe burns and alighted some of the rioter's hair on fire. The smell of burning hair, skin, and explosive gases was putrid causing some to gag, choke, while others regurgitated. Nearly everyone including the harbor police began running away from the source of the explosion causing some to be trampled on. Even Alex was hit by a small chunk of cement but not seriously injured.

Ho flagged down a taxi, and the two men made it back to their hotel safely. After a change of clothes and cleaning up in their rooms, they skipped checking out and hailed another taxi. It took them to the Hong Kong airport where they boarded a Cathay 757 that took them to Taipei, Taiwan. They were the first of the six-man team to arrive, and Lenten greeted them at the luggage turnstile.

Greater, Doc, Dennis, and Thomas were relaxing on the ship traveling from Kowloon Bay to Taipei. The China dolls with them were exhausted and mostly sleeping on reclining deck chairs. Despite their lack of makeup, most of them looked strikingly attractive even asleep. Long, silky black hair and closed almond eyes with slim nicely shaped bodies to match, they created a desirable scene for any man passing them on the deck of the ship.

The cruise was shortened a bit by the unusually calm waters. This enabled the ship to proceed at its near maximum knots allowing it to arrive in Taipei early on the next day. The dolls, now safe in an American-allied country, could seek asylum and citizenship here as political refugees. Some were trying to get to other countries; some were trying to contact their relatives in the PRC. They were given some Taiwan currency and left to choose their future.

Greater and the other three Americans took a taxi to the Taipei airport. Here, waiting many long hours for them by the baggage carousel, were Lenten, Alex, and Ho. Lenten suggested they all go to the Taipei Gardens restaurant for dim sum. However, all six men passed and sought a warm shower and a long nap. So Lenten took them to check in at the Sheraton near the airport. They were so exhausted that Doc and Dennis were falling asleep in the elevator. Three rooms on the twelfth floor were now occupied by six weary men sound asleep within minutes.

After breakfast on the following morning, Lenten and the six men take the hotel shuttle to the Taipei airport. Lenten charges seven first-class tickets on his American Express card. He figures it's the least he could do for his kyokai soldiers after what they've experienced. Still weary from a restless night's sleep, most of the men fall asleep on the plane. Moderate turbulence doesn't even disturb their slumber. Flying back to a radically different time zone at Newark airport (EWR) leaves them jet-lagged and walking like zombies on the tarmac. Lenten summons a stretch limo to take them back to the Hawthorne dojo where their vehicles are parked. Reconstruction of the training dojo has already begun but is unavailable for use.

The HPD building is adjacent to the dojo. Lenten leads them past the HPD receptionist into the secure conference room there. Each team gives a short verbal report of their mission. Lenten ensures that no recordings or notes are taken. It never happened. The team then disperses in the direction of each of their home bases. Lenten takes the limo back to EWR and departs for Okinawa where his Asian wife and family reside. He retired there after ten years being stationed in a Marine Corps base on the islands.

EPILOGUE

In China, Ping has heads rolling, and many executions take place. He doubles all the Imperial Palace guard posts. There is no news coverage in the PRC of the American's intrusion into his compound. As he plays with his two large-breasted concubines, he contemplates resetting up the China doll program. Unfortunately, during foreplay and a large hit of opium, Ping has myocardial infarction causing his death and the death of the China doll program.

In the Middle East, Dr. Ho is now teaching thermodynamics in Saudi Arabia at an astounding salary. He married his Filipina girlfriend and has three boys to raise with her.

Thomas retires to the Florida sunshine and gives private lessons in self-defense. His wife and family live with him there.

Greater returns to Arizona where he enjoys his retirement with his son and grandson. He is still packing a concealed Ruger .357 magnum wherever he goes.

Dennis opens a third karate dojo in Cliffside Park where many Koreans and Japanese have settled.

Doc goes back to Morris Medical Center where he is the chief surgeon of dentistry.

Alex, free of further threats to his life, decides to not pursue Chinese women any longer. He marries a Filipina on the advice of his lifelong friend and brother, Ming Ho.

The Van deGraff brothers, who assisted Lenten in Taipei, help rebuild the Hawthorne dojo and continue to work out there.

QED Alan Peters

ABOUT THE AUTHOR

Alan Peters, pen name of Al Piechowski, is a graduate chemist, senior product development engineer, and adjunct professor of chemistry and criminalistics. This story is based on real experiences with multiple fictitious enhancements. He resides with his Filipina wife in Califon, NJ.

The Author

CPSIA information can be obtained
at www.ICGtesting.com
Printed in the USA
LVHW111807140123
736912LV00003B/433